D0122357

Hoodoo

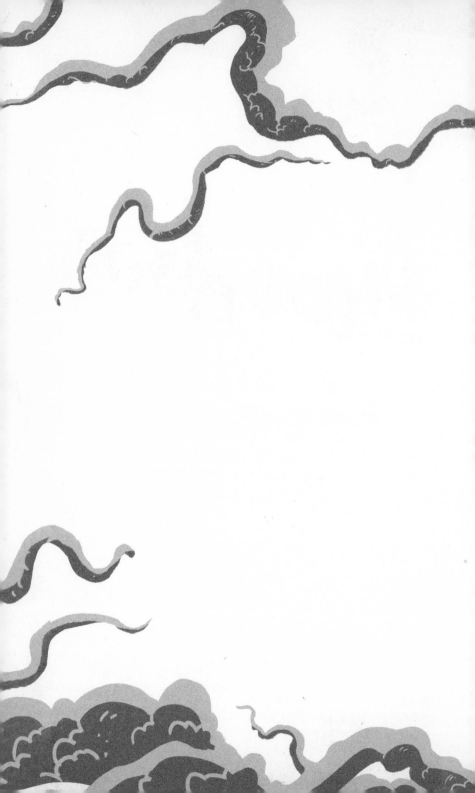

Hoodoo

Ronald L. Smith

CLARION BOOKS
Houghton Mifflin Harcourt
Boston   New York

Clarion Books
215 Park Avenue South
New York, New York 10003

Clarion Books is an imprint of
Houghton Mifflin Harcourt Publishing Company.

www.hmhco.com

The text was set in Carre Noir Std.
Design by Lisa Vega
Illustrations by Sebastien Skrobol and stock images from Shutterstock.

Library of Congress Cataloging-in-Publication Data is available.
ISBN 978-0-544-44525-3

Manufactured in the United States of America

DOC 10 9 8 7 6 5 4 3 2 1
4500546946

For my parents, Henry and Rose Smith,
who prepared me for the future by showing me the past.

CONTENTS

Hoodoo

The Stranger

When I got born, Mama Frances took one look at me and said, "That child is marked. He got hoodoo in him."

And that's how I got my name.

Hoodoo.

Hoodoo Hatcher.

She was talking about the red smudge under my left eye, shaped just like a heart. Not like a real heart I saw in a book one time, with blood pumping through it and all kinds of other stuff, but a heart somebody would carve in a tree with two names inside it.

Everybody said my birthmark was some kind of sign, but what it meant, nobody knew. I'll tell you one thing, though. People knew I was different as soon as they looked at me.

Mama Frances was my grandmama and she was the one

who raised me. My real mama died when I was born. My daddy died when I was five years old. I didn't know what happened to him, but Mama Frances said he ran off and came to a bad end. Supposedly he went and put a curse on a man in Tuscaloosa County, but I didn't believe that. I didn't think I'd ever know the real truth.

The sun was just starting to set and I needed to get back home. I'd been collecting stuff in the woods all day and my stomach was rumbling. I headed down the path, kicking up dirt clods along the way. Some bottle flies buzzed around my head, and I had to run a little bit to get them off. I called them greenies because I saw a dead one on the porch one time and its body was all green and shiny, like a piece of colored glass.

Something good-smelling came drifting through the woods. Mama Frances must've been cooking up some Hoppin' John. Hoppin' John is black-eyed peas and rice, if you didn't know. She made it all the time and I loved it.

Back home, I pulled the door shut and put my pillowcase bag on the kitchen table. It was full of rocks, pecans, some old bottle caps, a broken piece of chain, flattened pennies from the railroad tracks, and the skull of a baby bird I'd found under a tree.

Mama Frances eyed the bag on the table. "You know that don't belong there, child." She stood over the old stove, her smooth forehead dotted with beads of sweat. It was hot out, the middle of June, and even hotter in our house. I picked up the bag and set it on a chair.

"Not there either, Hoodoo. Upstairs. In your room."

Not everybody had an upstairs in their house. Most folks had one big room with a coal stove and an outhouse in the back. An outhouse is where people go to do their business, if you didn't know.

The reason we had an upstairs was because my granddaddy used to live here with Mama Frances, and she'd wanted a whole bunch of children. His name was Emanuel Hatcher. People had to call him by his first and last name or he wouldn't answer. He'd just sit there and pretend like he didn't hear you. I called him Pa Manuel, though, and he seemed okay with that. He didn't live with Mama Frances anymore because she said he was ornery as a yellow dog, so he moved out. I didn't see how somebody could have enough money to buy two houses but I guessed he did.

Mama Frances never did get all those children. The only child they'd had was my daddy, Curtis Hatcher. That made them my grandparents on my dead daddy's side. I was an only child too. Mama Frances said my real mama died because she didn't eat enough white clay when I was in her belly. I asked her why somebody would eat white clay, and she said it helped ladies have babies. That just sounded plain crazy to me.

I grabbed my bag and headed up the steps, keeping my eyes right in front of me. I didn't want to look at the picture of my family on the wall because it gave me the shivers. The reason it gave me the shivers was because when I looked at it, my great-aunt Eve stared at me with eyes that blazed like fire. Sometimes

I thought I saw her lips move, like she was trying to talk to me. The picture was old and wrinkly and the wooden frame around it was falling apart. There was some fancy handwriting on the bottom, and this was what it said:

Hatcher Family
Sardis, Alabama, 1919

Mama Frances said a white man came out to the country one time to take a picture of the whole family. It looked like a right nice day, because the sunshine was coming down through the leaves, making shadows on the ground. Everybody had put on their best church clothes and stood real still. My daddy was in that picture, standing between Mama Frances and Pa Manuel. This was before he married my mama. A tall hat sat on top of his head. Sometimes I'd stare at his face and ask him what he did that got him killed. He never answered, though. He just looked at me with those dark eyes of his until I had to turn away.

Most of the folks in that picture were dead now, buried over at Shiloh Baptist Church. Mama Frances called them "our people," and they all used hoodoo, or folk magick, as most people called it. They used foot-track powder that could go up through your foot and make you sick, a black hen's egg for getting rid of evil spirits, nutmeg seeds for good luck at gambling, and all kinds of other things.

But even though Mama Frances named me Hoodoo, I

couldn't cast a simple spell. I said the words over and over like she told me to, but nothing ever happened. "You got to believe, boy," she'd say. "That's the first step. *Believing.*"

I thought I did believe, but I guess I wasn't trying hard enough.

Everybody else in my family could conjure, though. Conjuring is using words to cast a spell, if you didn't know. One way to do it was by using a mojo bag. A mojo bag is a little cloth sack stuffed with roots and herbs and oils and sometimes a picture of somebody's face or words written on paper. Mama Frances gave me one that was supposed to be for good luck, but that didn't stop people from picking on me. Jessie McGuire, Otis Ross, and J.D. Barnes called me Hoodoo Doo-doo every time they saw me. They said I must've been cursed because of my birthmark. "Somebody put their mark on you," they'd said. "You got the evil eye."

But it was summertime, and the schoolhouse was closed, so I didn't have to worry about being picked on for a while.

Upstairs, I took all the stuff I found and put it in an old steamer trunk that used to be my daddy's. There was some writing on the side that said *20th Century Limited.* I figured that had to be some kind of train. Each corner of the trunk had a brass cap, and if you wanted to open it, you had to unfasten some wide belts and click a bunch of locks. I liked the sound it made when it opened. It'd give a big old groan, and the smell would rise up and greet me. I didn't know what that smell was, but it always made me think of my dead daddy.

I picked up the bird skull and turned it over in my hand. It was a tiny little thing, bone-white and clean. *What could've happened to it? Did it fall out of its nest? Did its mama try to save it?* I tucked it in a corner of the trunk on top of some old papers and then headed downstairs for some of Mama Frances's Hoppin' John.

I dragged the broom across the floor, tidying up in the back room of Miss Carter's store. Big bags of rice, flour, and sugar were heaped on stacks of wood, and boxes of candy lined the shelves. I didn't know who Miss Carter was and didn't think anyone else did either. Most of the time there was a blind man who ran the counter out front. He knew right where everything was, and if you tried to cheat him he'd know it. Somebody said he could tell the difference between a five-dollar bill and a one just by feeling it. I didn't know about that. I'd never even seen a five-dollar bill before, anyway. To tell you the truth, he gave me the heebie-jeebies.

My cousin Zeke worked at Miss Carter's once in a while and let me sweep up to earn some pocket change and candy. People came to buy groceries, tobacco, liquor, and medicine, but in the back—if you knew how to ask for it—you could get stuff for conjuring. I was more interested in the Mary Janes and hard candy under the glass counter out front.

Hot air blew in from the open window and sent dust balls floating around the room. I was playing make-believe that they were big twisters when the cowbell on the front door clang-a-langed. I stopped sweeping and peeked my head around the open door.

"Mornin', sir," I heard Zeke say. "How can I help you this fine day?"

I crept a little closer and saw a man standing at the counter. He was dressed all in black, like some kind of holy-roller preacher. His wide-brimmed hat shaded his eyes, and his long cloak trailed on the floor. I knew it was called a cloak because I saw one in a book at the schoolhouse. People used to wear them all the time in the olden days. I wondered why somebody would wear a cloak in this hot-ass weather. I wasn't supposed to say "hot-ass," but that's what popped in my head because I heard Mama Frances say it one time when she was fanning herself.

The man leaned forward, and I could've sworn I heard a creaking sound, like he was made of something besides flesh and bone. A cold chill crept across the back of my neck. I didn't like him, whoever he was.

"Mandragore," he said. His voice was so deep it boomed inside my chest.

Zeke cocked an ear in the stranger's direction. "What's that, now?"

The stranger looked up and sniffed, just like an old coon dog. "The One That Did the Deed," he muttered. *"Main de Gloire."*

Zeke backed up a step, like the man had stank breath. That was a sign that something wasn't right. Zeke shook his head. "Afraid I can't help you with that, good man. Never heard of it."

The man took one look around, sniffed again, and shuffled

out the store. He had to duck his head so his hat wouldn't get knocked off on the way out. The door banged shut, and the cowbell rang for what seemed like minutes.

Cousin Zeke laid his hands palm down on the counter and stood real still. Finally, he let out a big breath and took a hankie from his pocket. He wiped his face.

"Who was that?" I asked, coming around the corner.

Zeke jumped like he had ants in his pants. "Hoodoo! Don't be sneaking up on people like that!"

"I wasn't sneaking," I shot back. "I was here the whole time."

He balled up the hankie and put it back in his pocket. "Ain't nothing for you to worry about." He let out another breath and wiped his face with the back of his hand. "You better get yourself home for supper."

I'd never seen Cousin Zeke have a conniption before, but that's what it looked like. Having a conniption is when someone gets all jumpy, if you didn't know. He gave me a little half smile and reached in a jar for some Squirrel Nut Zippers.

"Here," he said. "Take some of these and have them after supper."

I held out my hand.

"And don't eat them on the way home. You hear?"

"Yes sir," I said.

I took the candy and stuffed it in my pocket.

On the way home, I wondered about the strange man and what he was looking for. I couldn't even remember the words he'd said. He walked funny too, like a big old bug. I'd seen a hat like the one he was wearing on a preacher man one time. But this stranger sure didn't look like no preacher. We knew everybody in town, and he wasn't one of them. I put him out of my mind and made my way on home. By the time I got there, I'd eaten all the Squirrel Nut Zippers.

"You been eating Zeke's candy, boy? What'd I say about eating all that sugar before supper?" Mama Frances scolded me with a shake of her head.

I stared at the food on my plate: big fat butter beans, a piece of bread, and a pork chop fried up in bacon fat. My stomach twisted.

"I only had a couple," I said.

"Mm, hmm," she said, smirking. "Boy, you better eat that food. Every bite."

She then proceeded to sit down and watch me clean my plate. It was good, but I felt my stomach getting bigger with every bite. By the time I was done, the sun was going down and I heard some night birds whistling.

Upstairs, I flopped down on the bed. My stomach hurt, like someone was churning up my insides with a big old spoon. I didn't remember falling asleep, but when I did, I had a dream. It was about that man from Miss Carter's store. Little dust devils swirled behind him as he shuffled down the street. He stood in front of me and opened up his cloak. I looked inside and saw the dried foot of a squirrel, a heart in a glass box, a bundle of twigs tied together with string, and a little bottle of hot pepper juice with a cork stopper. The man's eyes blazed with two red flames. "Mandragore," he said. A few long hairs poked out of his wide nostrils and his breath was bad. "The One That Did the Deed."

And that's when everything went black.

Jelly

I woke up the next day thinking about that dream. It gave me the willies. Why would I dream about that man at Miss Carter's store? It had to be him. He wore that same long cloak and smelled like he'd been in the fields all day, working up a stink.

How come I could smell him in a dream?

Mama Frances had to go into town to clean a white lady's house, so I was supposed to go to my Aunt Jelly's to do some chores. She was Mama Frances's little sister. I hated doing chores, but Aunt Jelly always made catfish, so I guessed it was worth it.

I sat down at the kitchen table. Mama Frances had left me a piece of corn bread and some salt bacon. I poured molasses all over the corn bread. Molasses is like syrup but thicker, if you didn't know. If you were a lazybones, and took forever to do something, people would say you were as slow as molasses.

Outside, the sun was high and bright and I had to squint right away. You can't look right into the sun or your eyes will burn out. I lifted the handle on the water pump, ducked my head under it, and took a long drink. Then I ran some water over my face. Mama Frances would've told me to use some soap. I didn't like soap, because for something that was supposed to make you clean, it smelled awful funny.

I crossed the railroad tracks and followed the path through the woods that led to Aunt Jelly's. I didn't know why we called her Jelly. People also called her Honey. I guess they did that because she was sweet.

I picked up a stick and whacked at an old rotten tree stump. A bunch of black beetles and spiders skittered out and I took off running. I didn't want no spiders getting on me. Aunt Jelly said a spider could go inside your ear and lay eggs. I poked inside my ear to make sure none had gotten in there.

I kept walking and saw some deer tracks leading off into the deeper part of the woods. Cousin Zeke taught me how to read tracks when I was little. I think he showed me how to do it because I didn't have a daddy.

It'd rained the night before, and slugs and snails slithered along the ground. I stepped over some big old mushrooms, all wet and soggy. The woods got real thin, and the next thing I knew, I was walking up the little white steps that led to Aunt Jelly's door. I knocked, and a minute later, it creaked open on rusty hinges.

"Hoodoo! How you doing, child?"

"I'm okay, Auntie."

Aunt Jelly was a pretty woman with dark curly hair and a gold tooth that sparkled in the sun. She always wore nice dresses, with bright colors and pictures of flowers.

"Come give your auntie some sugar," she said, leaning down.

I felt foolish but went ahead and kissed her on the cheek. She had on a whole bunch of perfume and it got all over me. Now I was gonna smell like a lady all day.

Inside, I got a big whiff of fried catfish up my nostrils. Aunt Jelly made the best catfish in the world. But don't tell Mama Frances I said that.

Aunt Jelly told me to sit down and then walked into the little kitchen. I could hear the hot grease popping and sizzling. "Got a whole mess of fish comin' right up, Hoodoo," she called. A mess means a bunch of fried fish, if you didn't know. You couldn't say "a mess of chicken." That just wouldn't be right.

My mouth started watering. Her catfish was crispy on the outside and soft and flaky on the inside. And even though I'd just had breakfast, I was still hungry.

I sat down at the dining room table. Aunt Jelly always had her table set for guests, with napkins sewn from bed sheets, vases stuffed with red roses, and what she called her fine silver lying next to big white china plates. She also had a chifforobe in the living room with nice coats hung up in it. There was a bottle of moonshine back there, too. Moonshine is homemade liquor, if you didn't know. I wondered why they called it moonshine. How could somebody get light from the moon and put it in a bottle? One time I snuck a drink and had to spit it out because my throat felt like it was on fire. When Aunt Jelly found out, she made me wait ten minutes before giving me a glass of buttermilk to cool down. It was the longest ten minutes ever. I promised myself I'd never drink liquor again after that.

The railroad tracks ran right behind Aunt Jelly's house, and I liked to sit out there sometimes and watch the trains rumble by. They had names like *Silver Maple* and *Frisco 1062*. At night-time, little sparks shot off the tracks from the wheels running over the rails. I played make-believe that those sparks were falling stars, shooting down from heaven.

When Aunt Jelly wanted to make some money, she'd cook up barbecue for the railroad men who came through town. She made the best barbecue sandwiches in the county. She'd put cracklin' right on top of the juicy meat, so when you took a bite, you'd get a big old crunch. Cracklin' is the dried skin of a pig, if you didn't know.

Aunt Jelly came into the dining room with a big plate of catfish and set it down on the table. I reached for a piece.

"Hoodoo," she warned.

My hand froze over the plate.

"Let it cool first, baby."

I put my hands in my lap. Aunt Jelly sat down. "Now go get that pitcher of sweet tea out of the kitchen."

I got up and tried not to roll my eyes. She was messing with me. Making me wait for that dang fish. One time she caught me rolling my eyes and told me they'd get stuck like that if I kept it up, so I didn't do it again.

I came back with the tea and took my seat. My eyes wandered to the catfish.

"Lay your napkin down," Aunt Jelly told me. "Remember how I showed you?"

I unrolled a napkin and put it across my knees.

"That's better."

My stomach gurgled. Aunt Jelly folded her arms across her bosom. "How's my sister?" she asked. "She don't come by to see me as much as she used to."

"She's okay," I replied, eyeing the plate. "She's at work."

Aunt Jelly leaned back in her chair and let out a breath. "Lord, those people gonna work your poor grandmama to death one day."

It was true. Sometimes it seemed like Mama Frances spent more time at white folks' houses than ours.

"Let's eat, baby," she finally said.

I didn't like that she called me "baby," but she called everybody that, even if they were grownups.

I put a few pieces of catfish on my plate and took a bite right away. It had cooled down, and the flaky white meat melted in my mouth. "That's good, Auntie," I said.

She cocked her head. "Now, what'd I say about talking with your mouth full, Hoodoo Hatcher?"

"Sorry," I said, still chewing.

She smiled like she was just teasing and picked up a piece herself. We sat there and ate without saying a word.

When my belly was fit to burst, she made me do some chores. I didn't want to fuss about it because the catfish she shared with me was so good. We worked together in her little garden where she grew some vegetables. If it was green and came out of the ground, we just called them greens. You could have mustard greens, turnip greens, collard greens, cabbage greens, and probably some other kind of greens I'd never even heard of. Once they were boiled up and got all soft, you could drink the water left in the pot. Mama Frances called it pot likker.

We picked the greens, washed them off, and put them in a brown paper bag for storing. After that, Aunt Jelly made me paint her door frame out front. She kept her eye on me the whole time to make sure I didn't spill any paint. I knew she could've done the chores herself, but she wanted me to do them because nobody got something for nothing. Especially catfish.

After I was done, I cleaned the brushes and washed my hands, then sat down to play a game of hearts. Hearts was the only card game I knew how to play, and I think Aunt Jelly let me beat her half the time. People thought I had some kind of special gift when it came to hearts because of my birthmark, but if I did, it was news to me.

Aunt Jelly smoked a little cigar and poured herself a glass of moonshine. She put some scratchy records on the wind-up player and closed her eyes and sang along. I liked when she sang "Minnie the Moocher" by a man named Cab Calloway. I didn't know who Minnie the Moocher was, but I liked the way those words sounded together: *Minnie the Moocher. Who was Minnie? What was mooching?*

We played until it started to get dark out. I heard some crickets and a train whistle in the distance. Finally, Aunt Jelly's eyes began to droop a little and she showed me out. She stood in the doorway, and the light from the moon made her thin flowery dress kind of see-through. I turned away.

"Tell your grandmama don't be a stranger," she called as I headed down the path.

"I will," I said.

I took a few steps.

"Hoodoo?"

I turned around. "Yes ma'am?"

"You been trying to conjure, baby?"

"No ma'am."

She nodded her head slowly, like she was thinking. "Well, give it time, child. It'll come when it's supposed to. Remember what your Mama Frances said?"

"I got to believe."

"That's right. Only believe. All have sinned and fallen short of the glory of God."

"Yes ma'am," I said, turning back around. Once Aunt Jelly started her Bible talk, I'd never be able to get away.

I set off and crossed the railroad tracks. Lightnin' bugs flickered in the growing dark, and night creatures rustled around in the woods. Owls hooted from their perches, possums slunk through the underbrush, and I'm sure snakes were creeping around too, looking for moles and other little animals. I took a deep breath. The air smelled like sweet sassafras.

And that's when I heard the scream.

My feet froze to the ground.

It was definitely a scream—a woman's scream—way in the distance. Hair rose up on the back of my neck.

"Lord, Jesus!" the voice rang out.

I got real scared right then. It sounded like it was coming from back where Aunt Jelly lived.

Aunt Jelly!

I took off running. It was dark, but I could still see by the light of the moon. I ran so fast I fell down and got right back up again. Some dogs must've heard me running, because they got to barking all of a sudden. A whole bunch of them—howling at the moon, Cousin Zeke would've called it. By the time I reached Aunt Jelly's, I was out of breath. I ran up the little steps and banged on the old wooden door frame. The paint was still wet, and it got on my hands. "Aunt Jelly! Aunt Jelly!" I shouted between gasps. She didn't answer, so I pushed open the door and ran inside. The front room was dark and I smashed my toe into a table. A creak sounded on the steps. I whipped my head around.

"Hoodoo?"

Aunt Jelly came down the stairs, pulling her robe around her. "What is it, boy? You scared me half to death."

She looked real plain because she'd taken off her lipstick

and earrings. "I heard somebody scream," I said. "Out by the railroad tracks. I thought it was you."

She didn't say anything for a second, just stared at me and put her hand on her hip. "Well, as you can see, Hoodoo, I'm as right as rain."

She leaned down and looked me in the eye. "You sure it was a scream? Maybe somebody killed a pig."

I felt foolish but I'd definitely heard a scream. I just knew it. I didn't say anything, just stared down at the floor.

"Sit down, baby," she said. "Let me make something to put your mind at ease."

I sat down on the couch. Aunt Jelly went into the kitchen, and after a few seconds, I heard drawers being pulled open and a spoon clinking around in a glass. She came back out holding a cup in both hands. "Auntie Jelly's hot toddy will set you straight," she said.

She placed the hot cup in front of me. Aunt Jelly knew a whole lot about potions and what she called elixirs. I put my nose to the cup and sniffed. The smell was so strong I was afraid to drink it. I remembered what happened the last time I drank some of her liquor. I didn't want to get that feeling again. "Don't be afraid, baby," she said. "It'll just calm your nerves. Make you right sleepy."

I picked up the cup and took a small swallow. I was surprised it tasted good—warm and buttery and sweet and creamy all at once. Aunt Jelly stared at me while I drank it. "You look just like your daddy. You know that, Hoodoo?"

"No," I said. I didn't want to think about my dead daddy.

I drank some more and pretty soon felt a little sleepy. Aunt Jelly sat on the couch next to me. She put a cool hand on my forehead. She started singing a song right then, but the words kind of floated away as she sang. I saw a picture in my head of me sitting under a tree in the sunshine. I was on a little hill by the Alabama River. Everything was quiet. The sun beat down on my neck. I dangled my bare feet in the cool water and splashed my toes. It felt good. I raised my face to the sun, but then the air got cold all of a sudden. A dark cloud passed overhead, leaving trails of black vines snaking down to the ground. The vines turned into long skinny fingers. They were trying to reach me — trying to creep along the ground and then come up and strangle me!

"Hoodoo?"

I shook my head back and forth, trying to wake up.

"*Hoodoo!* Wake up, child!"

I opened my eyes. My mouth was dry. I didn't know where I was for a second until I saw Aunt Jelly. She tried to pull me to her bosom like she did when I was little, but I wasn't little anymore.

She looked down her nose. "You think you're too big for one of your auntie's hugs?"

I didn't answer. I was thinking about that cloud that turned into a creeping black vine. She picked up my empty cup and sniffed it. "Auntie Jelly's hot toddy might be a little too strong!" she said, and then laughed.

And then I remembered why she gave me the drink in the first place. She was trying to calm me down. I'd heard a scream—a scream that sent shivers down my spine and tickled the hair on the back of my neck. She'd said it was probably a pig.

She was wrong.

That scream wasn't no pig.

That scream sounded like a human being.

THREE

Fate Revealed

I woke up with my sheets soaked through. For a second I thought I'd peed the bed, like when I was little, but then breathed a sigh of relief. It was only sweat.

Birds were singing outside my window. A little beam of sun came through and warmed my face. It felt good, but then I remembered the scream I'd heard last night and got scared. I thought it was a lady's scream, but now I wasn't so sure. I could still taste that potion Aunt Jelly made me drink in the back of my throat. My head felt foggy, too.

The smell of hot biscuits got my stomach to rumbling, so I threw on some clothes and headed downstairs. Mama Frances was stirring a big pot of grits on the stove. Grits are like rice but creamier, if you didn't know. I pulled out a chair and sat down.

"Hey, Hoodoo," she said.

"Mornin', Mama Frances."

"You go ahead and dig into those biscuits. Miss Ross just dropped off some fresh jam."

I picked up a biscuit and started to spread a little jam on it. "Ow!" I cried out.

I dropped it real quick and stuck my fingers in my mouth.

Mama Frances laughed. "That's what you get for not saying grace," she teased.

I closed my eyes and put my hands together. "Dear Lord," I said, "thank You for this food we are about to receive to nourish our bodies. In Jesus's name. Amen." I opened my eyes.

"That's better," she said.

I picked up the biscuit again. It was cooler to the touch, so I spread some more jam and butter on it and then took a bite. I rolled the dough around, trying to chew and blow on it at the same time. Let me tell you, that biscuit was so good it melted right in my mouth. The little seeds from the jam got stuck in my teeth, though.

Mama Frances sat down and pushed a bowl of hot buttered grits across the table. Wisps of steam rose off it like little ghosts. "It's Colored Folks' Day at the county fair," she said.

They called it Colored Folks' Day because that's the only time we could go. If we tried to go any other time, we could get in trouble from white folks. I didn't think that was right, but Mama Frances said that was the way of the world, and there was nothing we could do about it.

She pursed her lips and blew on her spoonful of grits. "Maybe little Miss Bunny'd like to go. Would you like that?"

A warm tingling spread over my face. Me and Bunny Richardson used to play together when we were little, but now that we were growing up, we didn't play so much anymore. Plus, I was starting to get a funny feeling in my stomach when she stood too close.

"You want to go?" Mama Frances asked.

I didn't say anything for a minute, just stared into my bowl of grits, watching the pool of butter melt. I felt a lump in my throat.

She grinned. "You shy, Hoodoo? I'll tell Bunny's mama you'll meet her at the fair."

"No!" I said, and then realized I'd shouted.

Mama Frances narrowed her eyes. "Child, don't you raise your voice in this house."

I sunk down in my seat. "I'm sorry, Mama Frances. It's just—I don't know. I don't know if we're still friends."

The scowl fell away from her face. "Sure you are, baby. You just got to take the first step."

I spread a little more jam on the biscuit. It was dark and wet, like blood, and that made me think about the scream.

Maybe it *was* a pig.

One time, Cousin Zeke took me out to Mr. Haney's farm to buy some hog meat. The dead hog was strung up on a steel pole with a big old cut right down its belly. I felt bad for the hog, but

Zeke said it'd had a good life and people had to eat. He said nothing would be wasted. The meat, the bones, the guts—there was something to be made out of all of it. I guessed I didn't feel so bad after he said that.

"Hoodoo? You listening to me, child?"

"Yes ma'am."

"I said you got to take the first step."

"Okay," I said, but wondered what that first step would be.

After breakfast, I went outside. The sun blazed like fire and I started to sweat right away, so I sat under the pecan tree and let the shade cool me off. Sometimes, I threw rocks up into the high branches and watched the nuts rain down onto the ground. Mama Frances made pecan pie whenever I picked up enough. She made other kinds of pies too: fig, plum, peach, and apricot. Peach pie was my favorite. She kept the fruit in mason jars in the cool dark under the porch. Once they got all soft and squishy, she'd put them in a pie. If I could eat only one thing and had to decide between Mama Frances's pies and Aunt Jelly's catfish, I think I'd be in a whole lot of trouble.

I stayed out in the yard for a long time, smashing pecans up against the tree trunk. Once they were cracked open, I picked inside the shell so I could get all the little nuggets. I think I was being idle. That's what Mama Frances called it. Being idle means wasting time, if you didn't know. I was thinking about Bunny and the fair and wondering what we'd do there. But something else was bothering me too—that scream, and the way it floated through the trees and over the tracks, sending a chill across my neck. Just thinking about it gave me the shakes.

The county fair was set up by the old cotton gin mill and surrounded by woods with tall weeping willow trees. I called them long-beards because the stringy gray moss that drooped down to the ground looked like the long beards of old men.

It'd only taken me a few minutes to get to the fair. I knew all the little paths through the woods, and even though it was getting dark out, I didn't even think about the scream. I never did say anything to Mama Frances. She'd probably tell me I was letting my imagination run wild. Taking a flight of fancy, she called it. I decided to just leave it alone. Whatever it was, it didn't have nothing to do with me nohow.

I came out of the path through the woods and into the clearing. Some lights were strung up through the trees, blinking red, blue, yellow, and green. Little flags on poles snapped in the dry wind. The smell of sugary-sweet cotton candy rose on the air. There were other smells too: sour hay and horse doo-doo, fried chicken and catfish, roasted peanuts, and a bunch of other stuff all jumbled up together.

I jingled the change in my pocket. Mama Frances had given me a whole bunch of it and told me to have a good time.

Somebody screamed.

I snapped my head left—then right—then up above. A bunch of legs, like a big old spider's, dangled from a wheel going round in the sky. People screamed and laughed and threw their arms up in the air, acting right foolish. You couldn't get me on one of those things if you promised me a hundred Squirrel Nut Zippers.

"Hey, Hoodoo."

I turned around.

It was Bunny.

"Hey, Bunny."

We stared at each other a minute. I looked down at the ground and shuffled my feet. Time got real slow all of a sudden. I snuck a look at her.

Bunny smiled. "Well, let's go inside," she finally said, after I didn't say anything else.

I dug into my front pocket and fished out two nickels for the ticket-taker man. He handed me two orange stubs and I stuck them in my back pocket.

"My mama said Miss Frances said you wanted to go," Bunny said. "So I thought I'd join you." She smiled again, showing off her perfect white teeth. Her hair was tied in two pigtails. I got that funny feeling in my stomach and almost had to turn away. Bunny just looked right at me and waited for me to say something. I shuffled my feet again. My hands were sweaty. "I wasn't sure," I finally said, "that you wanted to be my friend anymore."

"What?" Bunny's mouth dropped open. "What's wrong with you, Hoodoo? What made you think that?"

I kicked a pebble. A cloud of red dust rose in the air. "I don't know. We don't play together anymore. Playing's for little kids anyway. Right?"

She put one hand on her hip, just like Aunt Jelly, and shook her head from side to side. "You are a silly boy, Hoodoo Hatcher. C'mon. Let's go."

I was glad she said that, because, to tell the truth, I still wanted to be her friend.

Peanut shells crunched under our feet as we got lost in the crowd. People were everywhere. Sometimes I forgot how many folks lived in our county. They were all shapes and sizes. Some of them were as light-skinned as white folks and some as dark as blackberries. "The darker the berry, the sweeter the juice," I heard Aunt Jelly say one time, but I didn't know what it meant.

We took a ride on the merry-go-round. When I was little, I was afraid of the horses' teeth because they looked so real. But I wasn't little anymore. Bunny climbed onto a silvery horse with green stripes, and I got on one behind her that was sunshine yellow. We sat there for a minute and then the music started up—all topsy-turvy and silly-sounding. Bunny screamed as we rode round and round in circles.

The music died down and the horses started turning real slow. I liked that better, to be honest. We climbed off and the ground started moving under my feet. Bunny twirled in a circle, her arms spread out. "That was fun, Hoodoo!"

I reached out and put a hand on one of the horses.

"You all right?" she asked.

"Yup," I said, but my stomach was heaving.

We set off in no particular direction and took in the sights. There was strange stuff everywhere: a man on tall sticks clomped by wearing stripedy red and white pants, a fire-eater blew out streaks of yellow flame, and a lady with ink drawings all over her body hammered a nail up her nose. *Why would somebody mark up their body like that? And how come there was no blood from the nail?* Bunny stared at the lady like it was the neatest thing she'd ever seen.

"What you wanna do now?" she asked.

She stood there looking at me like I had all the answers. I wasn't sure what to say. I still felt a little wobbly from the merry-go-round.

"Step right up! Prizes! Candy! Toys! Everybody wins something!"

I turned to the left. A man with an eye patch stood in front of a stall. A bunch of prizes were stacked up behind him. He clapped his hands together and shouted again. "Prizes! Candy! Toys!"

"Let's play," Bunny said, pointing to the game.

I sighed. I wasn't that good at shooting or throwing things. Cousin Zeke made a slingshot for me one time, but I never hit anything with it. He could take out a squirrel with one shot.

We walked over, and the man took my nickel with a grunt. He looked as mean as a snake in a barrel. I'd never seen a snake in a barrel before, but people said that sometimes. The man reached into a peach bucket full of little brown balls and fished one out. It was soft, like a pillow, but felt like buckshot was in it. I could hear the tiny beads rattling around.

The game had a bunch of big rings laying down flat with smaller rings inside them, so I guessed I was supposed to throw the ball and try to get it inside one of them.

"If I win," I asked Bunny, "what prize do you want?"

She hummed to herself a second and then pointed. "That one."

I followed her finger to a case stuffed with teddy bears, wooden toys, some boxes of candy, and a giant pink rabbit. *Figures,* I thought, *that a girl named Bunny would want a rabbit.*

I tossed the ball from hand to hand a few more times. I took aim. *Concentrate,* I told myself, just like Zeke had told me to do with the slingshot. I lowered my arm, counted to three, and tossed the ball underhand. I held my breath. It seemed to take forever until it hit the rim of a ring and clattered down, lost in a wooden maze that held up the whole game. I tried two more times but with no luck.

Bunny sighed. "That's okay, Hoodoo. I didn't want that dumb old rabbit anyway."

I knew she was just saying that to make me feel better.

The man looked at me and smiled. He had exactly one tooth in the center of his gums. "I thought you said everybody wins something," I said.

He spit a wad of brown tobacco in the dirt. "Sometimes," he said, chuckling. "Sometimes."

I shook my head. That just wasn't right. Pa Manuel said the carnival was full of cheats, and that a sucker was born every minute. I guessed that meant me.

Bunny wanted to see the Alligator Boy, so we headed that way. I didn't see how anyone could be part gator, but I still went along with it. We passed a pen where a bunch of prize pigs snuffled in the mud—big ones, with black spots standing out on their pink skin. "Uh-oh," Bunny said.

"What?"

J.D. Barnes and Otis Ross leaned over the little fence, making squealing sounds and throwing peanuts at the pigs. J.D. caught my eye and elbowed Otis. They both made sour faces in our direction and started to walk over. My bones shook in my pants. The next thing I knew, they were standing in front of us.

"Look who it is," said J.D. "Little Hoodoo Doo-doo."

"And his girlfriend," said Otis. "Funny Bunny. She your girl-friend, boy?"

Bunny gave them a look that could've stopped a bull in its tracks. "Go on," she said, flapping her hand like she was shooing away flies. "No one wants you here."

"Who's talking to you?" said J.D., and he took a step closer. He and Otis were both in the same grade as me, but they looked like half-grown men. J.D. was as big as a house and had a scarred-up nose like a mangy old dog. Otis was skinny but had muscles all up and down his arms.

I was scared but had to do something. If I could conjure, I could've taken care of them a long time ago. But I wasn't any good at conjuring.

I took a step sideways and stood in front of Bunny. J.D. looked at Otis and laughed. And then he turned back to me and poked me hard in the chest with two fingers. I fell to the ground, right in the mud. They both howled with laughter.

"You got doo-doo on you!" cried Otis.

"Yeah," J.D. chimed in. "You got doo-doo on you. *Hoodoo.*"

I stood up. Mud was all over my hands and backside. Cold and wet seeped through my pants. I wiped my hands on my knees, making the whole thing even worse.

"You are both so stupid!" Bunny shouted. She clenched her fists and sneered. I thought she was about to fight them on her own.

"Hey!"

Bunny's big brother, Ozzie, rose up in front of us. His arms were like tree trunks and his hands like two hammers. He reached for his belt. He had a steel bull on the buckle and was known for beating people's behinds with it.

J.D. and Otis both took off running like pigs after slop. Ozzie looked me up and down, frowning at my muddy clothes. He lowered his head. "You okay, Hoodoo?"

"Yes sir," I said.

I didn't know Ozzie too good. People said he was a boxer and carried something called a bowie knife. A raised dark line ran across his right cheek like a zigzag. I always wondered how he got that scar, since he was the one with the knife. He looked out to where J.D. and Otis had taken off running. "Boys ain't got the sense to pour piss out a boot," he muttered.

Bunny put her hand to her mouth and giggled.

Ozzie hitched up his pants and looked to his little sister. He bent down a little. "You okay, baby girl?"

She nodded.

He pulled a clean hankie from his back pocket and handed it to me. "Go ahead and wipe yourself off, Hoodoo."

I took the hankie and wiped my hands. It came away all wet and dirty. I felt right stupid in front of Bunny with mud all over my backside. I balled up the hankie and tried to give it back to Ozzie, but he looked at me like I was crazy, so I stuffed it in my pocket.

"Don't worry about those boys," he said. "They'll get what's coming to them."

I thought about that and wondered if I'd be the one to give it to them.

Ozzie touched the side of Bunny's face and then punched me on the shoulder. I think he was just being friendly, but I almost fell over. He grinned, and the scar on his cheek wrinkled. "You two get going," he said. "And stay out of trouble, Hoodoo."

I didn't say anything, but I nodded like I understood. I wasn't the one who started the trouble, so why was he saying that to me?

Once we were a few steps away, Bunny stopped and turned to me. "Thank you, Hoodoo," she said.

"For what?"

"For standing up for me, silly."

"Oh," I said. "That's okay."

"You still wanna see the Alligator Boy?"

I didn't feel like seeing no Alligator Boy. I just wanted to go home. If people saw my behind, they'd think I went and pooped myself.

"I don't know," I said.

Bunny gave me a little half smile. "It's okay," she said. "I think I'm ready to go, anyway."

I sighed inside. I'd ruined Bunny's fun. I didn't win that pink rabbit and I couldn't fight, either.

I rubbed my arms. It was cold all of a sudden. The air smelled like a copper penny. I looked up. The moon was moving through the clouds real fast. I always wondered how that happened. Was the moon moving or the clouds?

We started walking back the way we came in, past the merry-go-round and the game where I didn't win a prize. I couldn't do nothing right. The man with the eye patch smiled at me again, his one tooth sitting in his head like a little fence post.

Up ahead, a brown tent was pinned down to the ground by four wooden stakes. A sign with bright red letters was in front of it.

MRS. SNUFF
FORTUNE TELLER
YOUR FATE REVEALED
25 CENTS

"Mrs. Snuff," I whispered.

"You should do it, Hoodoo," Bunny said. "Get your fortune read. Maybe she'll say you're gonna grow up rich and famous."

I thought about that for a second. I didn't want to talk to no fortuneteller. She might say something about that scream or the dream I had with the strange man. I let out a deep breath and jingled the change in my pocket. I wasn't sure I had enough left for both of us, and I didn't want to go in anyway.

"That's okay," Bunny said. "You don't have to pay for me. I'll just watch. C'mon."

A man sitting on a bale of hay took my money. His lips moved in a funny way, like a cow chewing its cud. I pulled aside the flap of the tent and walked in. Bunny followed behind me.

The dirt floor smelled wet and musty, like moldy leaves. Red candles sat on stumps of wood, and a bunch of jars full of something all slimy were stacked in one corner. A tiny little woman sat hunched over a scarred wooden table. Bunny elbowed me in the ribs. "Go 'head, Hoodoo."

She must've been Mrs. Snuff, I figured. She was wearing a red robe, like she couldn't even bother to put on real clothes. She curled a long finger in my direction. I got the heebie-jeebies real quick but didn't want to look afraid, so I slowly walked over and sat on a wooden stool in front of her. Bunny stayed standing up beside me. It was so quiet, I didn't even hear all the people outside.

"What is your name?" the lady croaked, staring dead at me. One of her eyes was clouded over and looked all milky.

"Hoodoo, ma'am," I said. "Hoodoo Hatcher."

"From-across-the-river Hatchers," she asked, "or the city Hatchers?"

There were all kinds of Hatchers in our town—white Hatchers and black Hatchers and some that were black and white at the same time. I didn't know which ones we were, so I just said, "Emanuel Hatcher's Hatchers."

"I see," she said. "And what do you know about hoodoo . . . *Hoodoo?*"

I didn't answer. She took my right hand and turned it over. Her skin was brown and rough and crisscrossed with wrinkles. She looked like she was about a hundred years old.

"One hundred and *five*," she said with a wink.

I swallowed hard.

She let go of my hand. Her eyes traveled up my face and landed on my birthmark. "Where'd you get that mark, boy?"

"I don't know," I said. "I was born with it."

"Gotta have heart," she said, almost to herself. "Gotta have heart."

Right about then I felt like I wanted to get up and go, but Mrs. Snuff suddenly sat up straight, like she was stricken. "Darkness follows you," she said, her good eye going all wide.

"Your people," she went on, her old lips trembling. "They're in danger too. But their fate is in your hands."

The red candles all around us whooshed out. Bunny gasped. Chicken skin rose up on my arms.

"C'mon, Hoodoo," Bunny said. "We should go."

I started to get up, but Mrs. Snuff's old claw shot out and grabbed my left hand.

"Ow!" I cried, but she didn't let go. She closed her eyes. I saw the tiny veins on her eyelids standing out, like they were alive under her skin. She held on so tight her nails were digging into me.

"Search for the black crow," she said. "He will help you. Beware the Stranger."

I yanked my hand away and jumped up, knocking over the little wooden stool. I raced to the front of the tent and flung the flap open, with Bunny hot on my heels.

Once we were back in the crowd, Bunny took my hand and looked at it. "Did she hurt you?" she asked. "That lady's crazy!"

I pulled my hand away and rubbed the spot where Mrs. Snuff had grabbed me. "No," I said. "I'm okay." But inside, I was still shook up.

"What's she talking about?" Bunny asked. "What crow? Who's the Stranger?"

"I don't know," I said. "Just some crazy old lady, like you said."

But I wasn't so sure about that. *Was she talking about that nasty man at Miss Carter's—the same man I dreamed about? He was the only stranger I'd seen lately.*

"Hoodoo?" Bunny said.

"Yeah?"

"What's wrong?"

"Nothing."

But I could tell by the way she was looking at me she knew I was hiding something.

"Don't worry about that lady," she said. "She ain't right in the head, with her crazy old eyes. C'mon. Let's get some hush puppies. My treat."

That sounded good to me. Hush puppies are fried pieces of cornbread, if you didn't know.

It took us a little while to find the hush puppies man, but when we did, we sat down under a long-beard tree and shared them with an ice-cold Co-Cola.

"Your grandmama tell you what happened last night?" Bunny asked.

I licked my fingers, all sticky and greasy. "Nope."

"Somebody dug up some bodies at the graveyard."

"That's bad," I said. "Why would somebody do that?"

"I don't know," she said. "But my mama said Miss McGuire went by there last night to drop off some flowers, and that's when she saw it."

"Saw what?"

Bunny slurped from her straw, then looked up at me. "Their hands, Hoodoo. Somebody went and chopped off their hands."

FOUR

Dead Man Walking

I walked through the graveyard on my tiptoes, trying not to step on the graves. If you stepped on a grave, people said, the dead could steal your soul. I could barely see, and the only light came from the moon, spreading a glow through the long-beard trees.

Something kept tickling my face, like a spider's web. I brushed it away, but that didn't do any good. It was stuck there, creeping across my skin.

I was looking for Daddy's grave. I didn't know why, but I had to find it. The headstones on the graves were so old, I couldn't read the names.

I took a few more steps and stopped.

The ground was moving under my feet!

My head went dizzy, like I was back on the merry-go-round at

the fair. My mouth clamped shut. I saw something out of the corner
of my eye and turned.

A hand, followed by a long arm, shot right up out of the dirt.
Crooked black fingers grabbed at the empty air.

And then, with a sound like an ax chopping through wood, a
dead man rose up out of his pine box.

He had on a long cloak and a wide-brimmed black hat. His
eyes glowed red. He was coming for me. "Mandragore," he said, as
slow as molasses. "The One That Did the Deed."

"Aieeeeee!" I screamed, waking up.

Mama Frances rushed into my room in her nightgown,
swinging a kerosene lantern. "What is it, Hoodoo? What's
wrong, child?"

She sat down on the edge of the bed and set the lantern
on the floor. The thin mattress sunk under her weight. I had
to settle down for a minute to get my breath back. The dream
seemed so real. I touched my face to see if there were any spider
webs on it. "Bunny said somebody dug up some bodies at the
graveyard," I said all in a rush. "She said somebody chopped off
their hands!"

Mama Frances's eyes widened. "Hush now, child. That was
a terrible thing. No need for you to fret about it." She paused.
"Whoever did that is goin' straight to hell."

I was shocked. Mama Frances didn't usually say cuss words
in front of me, but I wasn't sure *hell* was a real cuss word because
Preacher Wellington said it in church all the time.

"Why would somebody do that?" I asked her.

She stroked my hand. "A lot of strange things in this world, Hoodoo, and only the Lord above knows the answer."

I thought about that. *Did the Lord really have the answers?* But then I got scared because, if He wanted to, the Lord could strike me down with a bolt of lightning whenever He felt like it.

"There was a lady at the fair," I said. "She said I was in danger. She said to look for a black crow and to watch out for the Stranger."

Mama Frances's head snapped back. "Who said that, Hoodoo? What lady?"

"A fortuneteller." I wiped my nose with the back of my hand. "Her name was Mrs. Snuff. Is something bad gonna happen?"

Mama Frances pursed her lips. *"Snuff,"* she whispered, like she might've known the name. She shook her head. "You just close your eyes and go back to sleep, baby. Ain't nothin' to fear here. We got the power of the Lord in this house."

She rose up off the bed and then bent down and looked me dead in the eye. "And other things too."

She picked up the lantern and closed the door behind her.

Darkness settled over the room.

I tossed and turned, making the blanket all scrunched up around me. I pulled it higher, all the way to my chin, even though the room was hot and stuffy. I tried to calm down but couldn't. My heart jumped around like a bird trying to get out of a cage.

Mama Frances told me one time that counting numbers was

a good way to get to sleep. "Count your numbers, boy," she'd said, "and you'll doze off in no time."

I closed my eyes.

I'd count to one hundred. That's what I'd do. I'd start counting and when I opened my eyes it'd be morning.

I let out a deep breath and turned on my side.

One . . . two . . . three . . . four . . .

I didn't remember falling asleep, but when I woke up the next morning, there was a broom lying across my doorway. I knew what that meant. It was a keep-away spell. And people used it to keep evil spirits from coming into their house.

FIVE

A Message on Wings

I put one leg in front of the other and stepped over the broom.

If Mama Frances thought there was nothing to be scared of, then why'd she put that keep-away spell in front of my door?

I had to protect myself. Mrs. Snuff said to beware the Stranger. The only stranger I'd seen was the man at Miss Carter's store, the same man who was in my dreams. *Was he the Stranger? What did he want with me?*

I thought back to the dream from the night before. Those words he said stuck in my head. They were the same words he said at Miss Carter's, all deep and slow-sounding: *Mandragore. The One That Did the Deed.*

What did it mean?

I'd have to ask Mama Frances. She'd know. She knew all about dreams.

I found her stirring some grits on the stove, like always.

"You get back to sleep last night, baby?" she asked.

"Yes ma'am. I counted my numbers like you said."

"Good," she said. "If you get tired of counting numbers you can count chickens, too!"

I thought that was right funny, but didn't feel like laughing.

She moved the pot of grits off the stove and set it on some square bricks pushed together. It had to cool a little before we could eat them. She pulled out a chair and sat down. "Whew!" she said, wiping her head. "Hot out, Hoodoo."

I looked at her. She was always standing, always on her feet.

"Mama Frances?"

"Yes, baby?"

"What's *Mandragore*?"

"*Mandragore*? What kind of word is that?"

"I don't know. You ever hear it before?"

"Where'd you hear this, Hoodoo? At the fair? Something that fortuneteller lady said?"

"No ma'am. It was in a dream."

Mama Frances got a real serious look and then tightened her lips. "Dreams are full of what we call symbols, Hoodoo, and they always tell you something you already know. Deep down inside. What else was in this dream?"

I looked at her hands. They were old and knobby, like

walnuts. They'd been that way for as long as I could remember.

"A man," I said. "He came up out of the ground and said that word."

She frowned, and her eyebrows went down. "That sounds like an omen. You remember what an omen is?"

"A sign," I said. "It can be good or bad. Right?"

"That's right, child. And I don't know which your dream is trying to tell you."

I swallowed hard.

"Mandragore," she whispered, shaking her head. "I'll ask your Pa Manuel about it. But I want you to promise me something."

"Yes ma'am?"

"I want you to come to me if you have any more dreams. You understand?"

"Yes ma'am," I said again.

I ate my grits with a big pat of butter on them. Mama Frances didn't ask me anything else, and by the time I was finished, she was putting on her white clothes to go clean houses.

Upstairs, I thought about what Mrs. Snuff had said: *Your people. They're in danger too. But their fate is in your hands.*

I didn't know what that meant. How could their fate be in my hands? Fate is something that happens that you can't do nothing about, if you didn't know.

Search for the black crow. He will help you. Beware the Stranger.

If I knew how to conjure I could put a spell on that stranger.

46

But I didn't know how. One time, Mama Frances was plucking a black hen because she needed the feathers to do some kind of conjure work. When she asked me to help, I couldn't, because every time I touched the feathers I got the shivers.

I dug my fingers into my pants pockets and pulled out some change. I had two pennies left from the fair. I bent down and stuck one in the heel of my shoe. I heard that was supposed to help keep evil away. I thought about the other things I heard my family talk about—laying down tricks and sprinkling powders—but I didn't know how to do all that.

I stuck my hands in my pockets and turned them inside out. That was supposed to help too. But I couldn't go around all day looking like that. People would think I was touched in the head. So I stuffed them back in.

I looked around my room. There wasn't a whole lot there. Just my bed, a bird whistle, some marbles in a cloth sack, Daddy's old trunk, and an end table with a Bible that I was supposed to read from every night, even though I didn't.

I chewed my lip. Right then I remembered something I'd heard Aunt Jelly say one time. She was showing me how to cook barbecue and was talking to a man named Cuz. I guess "Cuz" was short for "cousin." Anybody could be a cousin where I came from. All you had to do was come over and eat every day, and you could be a cousin. This man Cuz said somebody was after him and he needed some help. Aunt Jelly whispered and told him what to do. She didn't think I was listening, but I was. Maybe it'd work for me, too.

I opened the little drawer where the Bible was and reached inside for my pencil and paper from the schoolhouse. I wasn't supposed to use the paper because I needed it for when school came back, but this was something I had to do. I stuffed everything in my pillowcase bag and went back downstairs.

Mama Frances had put some fresh flowers on the little altar on the table at the foot of the steps. An altar is where you put things to help your dead family look over you, if you didn't know. Once your people died, they became something called ancestors.

There was a little toy Jesus, some red candles, some dirt in a bowl, a glass of water, and a ring with a painted eye on it. I wanted to pick it up but thought better of it. It was too big to be a lady's ring. Maybe it was my daddy's. Mama Frances must've put it there.

The smell of the flowers was sweet and made me a little sad for my dead daddy. I reached out and touched one of the little purple leaves. I closed my eyes. "Dear ancestors," I said. "Please look over me and Mama Frances. Please keep that stranger away from our door and send him back wherever he came from. In Jesus's name. Amen. Thank you."

I opened my eyes. "There," I said.

Outside, I had to dig around for a while to find a hammer and nail, but finally found them in a little steel box by the outhouse. I think Pa Manuel used that toolbox every now and then. He was always coming over to fix something. Once I had everything I needed, I set off on my way.

I passed by Miss Carter's store and saw Ozzie playing dominoes with some of the older men. I stopped to watch them, but they didn't even look at me. They just slammed their dominoes down on the table and shouted at one another like they were crazy. They were drinking liquor, too. I could smell it, sharp and strong. Drinking liquor was bad enough, but drinking it in the morning was just plain crazy.

Blue and purple wildflowers sprung up all around me the closer I got to the woods. I plucked a handful of strawberries from a little patch and popped them in my mouth. They were the sweetest strawberries I'd ever tasted, and I let the juice run down my chin. I felt a little bit of joy right about then, but it disappeared as soon as I looked at the red smudges on my fingertips because it made me think about blood.

I made my way through the woods, looking at each tree as I passed it. I needed to find a big one. The air was thick and muggy and little gnats flew around my head. I hated gnats.

One tree stood out from the others, with a wide trunk and gnarly arms stretched to the sky. I stood under it. The shady leaves cooled me off a little. I slung my pillowcase bag off my shoulder and sat down. Then I took out my pencil and paper. I closed my eyes and took a deep breath. The last thing I wanted to think about was that man—the Stranger—but I had to put a picture of him in my mind for the spell to work. I just hoped I had the right man. He was the only stranger I'd seen.

I put the pencil to paper and drew a circle shape for his head. That was the easy part. Then I added the hat. I started on the eyes next—black and evil-looking. The nose was just a dot and the lips two little lines pressed together.

I pulled my head back and looked at it. It didn't really look like him, but I figured it was close enough.

I took out my hammer and nail. With my left hand, I held the paper up to the tree, and with my right, put the point of the nail right on the Stranger's forehead. "One . . . two . . . three!" *Bam!*

I drove the nail right through the picture and into the trunk of the tree.

I dropped my hand. "There," I said. "Begone, you old stranger."

The corners of the paper fluttered in a breeze. I bent down to pick up my bag. When I rose back up and took another look, the Stranger's eyes were bleeding.

That ain't right. Somebody's playing tricks on me.

I stretched my neck out, like a snappin' turtle, trying to get a closer look. A bird squawked in the branches. I moved a little closer, my breath caught in my throat. It was just tree sap, leaking through the paper. "Fool boy," I said, just like Mama Frances would've. I chuckled a little, trying to put myself at ease. But it still gave me the willies.

I set off on my way back home. Soft green moss grew on the ground and made my feet sink in a little. I liked moss. It looked all sparkly when the sun hit it. One time I lifted a patch right out of the ground and brought it home, but Mama Frances told me to get that dirt out of her house.

A fly landed on the back of my neck and I slapped it away. Another one buzzed around my head at the same time. I waved that one away too. "Get outta here!" I shouted. But that only brought more flies, hissing and swarming. "Get off!" I cried, but the flies kept coming—big greenies, like a black cloud. They landed on my head and back, down in the little cracks of my too-big shoes, tickling my ears. They were everywhere!

I ran toward the river, the flies buzzing on my tail. I figured I might have to jump in to get them off, but by the time I got there, they were gone. I sat down and put my head between my knees, breathing hard. Sweat poured off my face. I didn't know if those flies were a good thing or a bad thing, but I didn't like it one bit. And even though they were gone, I still felt their ghosts on my skin.

I slumped back against a long-beard tree. The Alabama River flowed below me like a wide silver ribbon. I was on a little hill, and the shade made the sweat dry on my skin. If Mama Frances knew that, she'd make me take a bath when I got home.

A big old boat was out there, carrying chopped-up logs. Clouds of black smoke puffed from a hole in its top. I wondered what it would be like to jump on that boat and go wherever it was headed. *Where would it take me? What would I see?* I knew there was more to the world than our little town, but nobody I knew had ever been outside it.

Some dragonflies floated over the water, their wings flashing like red- and green-colored glass. One time, a man brought something to the schoolhouse called a kaleidoscope, and when I looked through it, a bunch of colors swirled around. That's what the dragonflies' wings made me think of.

It was nice and cool under the tree, and I felt like I could've fallen asleep right there. *Dang flies,* I thought. *That was crazy.* Now that I'd nailed that stranger's picture to the tree, he couldn't get to me. There were probably some words to go with that spell but I didn't know them. I closed my eyes and stretched my feet out in the cool dirt. Sweet sassafras drifted on the air.

"Hoodoo."

I jumped up, wide awake.

"Who's there?" I called to the air. It was quiet for a minute, except for the sound of a boat in the distance, chugging its horn.

"Hoodoo," the voice called again.

I pushed myself up on my elbows, looking left, then right. I couldn't tell if it was a man's or a woman's voice, but it was kind of high and reedy. Hair rose on the back of my neck. I looked around. It was quiet for a minute, and then a black shape swooped down from the tree in a flutter of feathers. It was a crow, a big one, with eyes as black as the devil's. Leaves and twigs fell onto my head.

"Caw! Caw!" the crow squawked. "Don't fear me, child."

I blinked and jumped back, then swallowed. "How do you . . . how can you talk?"

The bird buried its beak in its blue-black feathers. "Danger comin', Hoodoo. I was sent by your daddy. From the crossroads. He's stuck."

"My daddy? What do you mean, 'stuck'? What crossroads?"

"The crossroads, boy," the crow said, like I was supposed to know what it was talking about. "You gotta set something right for him, or he can't pass on."

"How can you talk?" I asked again, not even believing I was talking to a bird that knew my name. And then I remembered Mrs. Snuff's words: *Search for the black crow . . . Beware the Stranger.*

"I'm a spirit, boy," the crow said. "From the other side."

"A spirit?"

The crow stuck its beak in the wet dirt. When it came back up, a fat worm dangled at the end of it.

"What am I supposed to do?" I asked.

"There's a bad man in town," the crow said. "A demon. He's dead and alive at the same time. If you don't stop him, he'll bring terror and darkness on your people." It gulped down the worm. I had a vision of the dead man rising out of his pine box. *Mandragore. The One That Did the Deed.*

I thought I was going to be sick. A dark cloud passed over the sun. My arms got cold all of a sudden.

"So what's my daddy want me to do?"

"Ack!" the crow screamed. "You gots to kill him, Hoodoo."

"Who?"

"The bad man," the crow squawked. "The Stranger."

"What?" I shouted. "I can't kill nobody. That's crazy!"

"If you want to help your daddy pass on, you gots to."

"How?" I asked. "How am I supposed to kill somebody?"

The crow cocked its head. I swear the dang bird winked at me. "I don't know, boy. That's for you to figure out, ain't it?"

And with that, it let out a cry and flew into the air, its wings as loud as a clap of thunder.

Crossroads

I ran home, jumping over logs and dashing through fields of cattails, slipping in patches of wet mud. Thorny brambles stung my ankles but I didn't feel a thing.

Mrs. Snuff was right. I found the crow—or it found me— and it said to beware the Stranger, too. *Just like she did!*

It was the man at Miss Carter's store. It had to be. He was the same man I dreamed about. *The same man who rose up out of that pine box!*

I swung the door open and rushed inside. Mama Frances was snapping green beans at the table. "There a fire somewhere, Hoodoo?" she asked without even looking up.

"No ma'am," I said, and suddenly thought I'd dreamed the whole thing. But then I saw the crow's shiny black eye in my mind and knew it really happened.

"I saw a crow," I said. "It talked to me."

Mama Frances stopped her snapping. She looked up. She must've thought I was crazy. "Did you actually hear the words out loud, Hoodoo, or in your head?"

I had to think about that. I knew that dang bird talked to me, but the more I thought about it, I wasn't sure. "I think it was out loud," I said. "It said that Daddy was stuck in the crossroads and I needed to help him pass on."

Mama Frances pressed her lips together.

"What's the crossroads?" I asked. "Mama Frances, how can a bird talk?"

She threw the last bean she'd snapped into the pot. "Sit down, Hoodoo," she said.

I pulled out a chair and sat. Mama Frances let out a breath. "Where were you when you heard this?"

"Down by the river. I was just sitting there watching a big old boat go by. I fell asleep, and then this crow came down from the trees and started talking to me."

She closed her eyes and opened them again. "You sure it said 'crossroads'?"

"Yes ma'am."

"Well, child, the crossroads is the place where heaven and hell meet. It's where people get stuck when they have to finish business in the living world. It's also a place where two roads cross at a right angle, and where powerful mojo can be done, but it's dangerous, because the old devil himself can sometimes rise up and cause confusion."

I didn't like the way that sounded, and it made me right scared.

"What else did this crow say?"

My left hand started itching and I scratched it.

Mama Frances raised an eyebrow. "What's wrong, child? Why you scratching your hand like that?"

She took my hand in hers and turned it over.

"Just itching," I said.

She dropped my hand and fixed her eyes on me. "You been trying to conjure, boy? Something you been messing with?"

"No ma'am."

"You just be careful," she said. "You hear me?"

"Yes ma'am."

"If you see that crow again, I want you to come straight to me. You understand?"

I nodded.

She started snapping beans and throwing them into the pot. "Now go out back and get some firewood. I'll cook these beans for supper."

I got up and went outside. The firewood was all stacked up behind the house. I wasn't big enough to swing the ax, so Pa Manuel had to come over to do it now and then. He said stacking the wood right was just as important as chopping it. I bent down and picked up a few pieces.

I gulped.

Underneath that wood, a bunch of fat black worms were wriggling around in the dirt.

. . .

Mama Frances made fried chicken to go with the green beans for supper, but I wasn't hungry. I was thinking about that old black crow and the man called the Stranger.

Danger comin', Hoodoo. I was sent by your daddy. From the crossroads. He's stuck.

What did my daddy want with me? Mama Frances said he came to a bad end. I didn't want that to happen to me. And I didn't want no parts of his business, either.

I looked at the food on my plate. Mama Frances watched me like a hawk. I ate one chicken wing and a little bit of the beans she'd snapped. The crow's words—*the crow's words! How could a crow talk?*—floated around in my brain, and I couldn't get them out:

He's dead and alive at the same time. If you don't stop him, he'll bring terror and darkness on your people.

I went to bed right after eating. My dreams were full of black crows squawking and screaming. They flew into the house and blocked the windows so no light could come in.

And then I saw him.

The Stranger. He was standing by my bed. I tried to scream, but he opened his mouth so wide he swallowed the whole room with me inside it.

SEVEN

The Cliff

An old truck tire hung from a low tree branch and swung back and forth over the water. The Alabama River snaked down below us. We called this place the Cliff, because when you sat at the top of the hill you could see the whole town.

We weren't supposed to go swimming in the river because a boy named Jimmy got drowned there one time. He fell off the swing and they didn't find his body for three days. People said a gator took a big old bite out of him, but I didn't believe that. People just liked telling tales, Pa Manuel said. "Hoodoo," he told me, "most folks round here got both paddles on the same side of the boat."

I figured that meant Pa Manuel thought he was smarter than most people.

Bunny raced back up the hill and spilled a bunch of rocks

in front of me. She'd been carrying them in the lap of her dress. Her mama made her wear nice dresses, but Bunny'd get them dirty anyway. That's what I liked about her. She wasn't like the other girls at the schoolhouse. She did everything a boy did and some things even better. She knew how to toss horseshoes. She could run faster than me. And she knew how to play mumblety-peg. Mumblety-peg is a game where you have to throw a knife at somebody's foot and see how close you can get without sticking them, if you didn't know.

She bent down and picked up a rock. "Look at this one," she said, holding it up to the sun. "That's *gotta* be gold."

She handed it to me. Little flashes of light sparked inside it.

"I don't know about that, Bunny. Pa Manuel said white people took all the gold a long time ago."

Her face soured. She sat down beside me and dug her fingers in the pile of rocks, every now and then picking one up and looking hard at it.

I told her all about the crow, and she listened with wide eyes.

"A crow?" she said. "It talked to you? That's what that lady at the fair said. 'Search for the black crow.'"

"I know," I told her. "She said to watch out for a stranger, too."

Bunny got real quiet. "Did you *see* a stranger, Hoodoo?" she finally asked. "Somebody you thought wasn't right?"

"I saw a man at Miss Carter's a few days ago. He gave me the willies. All wrapped in black. I been seeing him in my dreams, too."

"That ain't good. You gotta tell somebody. What if that crow's telling the truth?"

I picked up a broken branch and flung it out over the water. I missed and hit a tree instead, sending a bunch of birds into a racket. "I don't know," I said.

"Get your Mama Frances to help," Bunny said. "She knows that magick your family does. And your Pa Manuel, too."

Bunny's family didn't use hoodoo, but they knew mine did. Everybody but me. Aunt Jelly told me I'd learn to conjure when the time was right. *What if the time was never right? What would I do then?*

I looked out at the river, thinking hard.

"Hoodoo?" Bunny asked. "You okay? What you thinking about?"

"Mrs. Snuff," I said. "Maybe she can help."

Bunny shook her head back and forth. "That lady's scary. With her crazy old eyes!"

"She was right about the crow," I said. "I need to find her."

"Fair's probably packed up and moved on."

She was right. After Colored Folks' Day, most fairs left town.

"Somebody's gotta know where she stays," I said.

"Well," Bunny said, still fiddling with her rocks, "if you find her, we can go see her together."

I chewed my lip and looked at the ground.

"What?" she asked. "What's wrong?"

"I think I have to go on my own."

"Why?"

I scratched in the dirt with a stick. "Mrs. Snuff said my family was in danger. Right?"

"Right."

"She said their fate was in my hands. That means *I* need to fix it. I don't want nobody getting hurt. Mama Frances or Cousin Zeke or Aunt Jelly."

Bunny got a look right then like she was proud of me.

"And you too, Bunny. I don't want you getting all mixed up in this."

My face got hot.

She smiled. "That is mighty brave, Hoodoo. That's what my daddy calls selflessness. You just let me know if you need me. Okay?"

"Okay," I said.

We sat there a little while longer, watching some blackbirds hop around on the tire swing and then fly away. A shiny fish splashed up in the air and then back down again, its scales gleaming like silver.

He's dead and alive at the same time. If you don't stop him, he'll bring terror and darkness on your people.

By the time we were ready to leave, dark storm clouds were rolling in—big black ones, with jagged strikes of lightning flickering inside them. Bunny picked up her rocks and tossed them down the hill.

EIGHT

A Bad Man's Song

Mama Frances scooped some grits out the pot and onto my plate. She sat down next to me and let out a big breath. She was tired. She was always tired, but never stopped moving. "No time to stand still," she'd say sometimes.

"I been thinking," she said. "That crow came to you for a reason, Hoodoo. Spirits don't just come to people and warn them about danger. You got some magick in you, but I think it's buried. Way down deep. That's why that bird was drawn to you."

"You really think so, Mama Frances? That I got some magick?"

"Could be," she said. "But there's something else, too."

"What?"

"That old crow could be a trickster."

"What's a trickster?"

"A trickster's got its own reasons for doing things. They can be double-crossers. Especially ravens and crows."

"Trickster," I whispered. I didn't like the sound of that.

"You just be careful, boy. You hear me?"

"Yes ma'am," I answered.

"Remember what I told you? If you have any more dreams or see anything that don't seem right, I want you to come straight to me. You understand?"

"Yes ma'am," I said again. I thought about the dream with the Stranger and the crows but didn't say anything.

Five minutes later I stuffed a biscuit in my pocket, grabbed my pillowcase bag, and headed out the door.

Like Bunny said, the fair was probably packed up, but I decided to try there first anyway. Mrs. Snuff had to know more about the crow and the Stranger. She was the one who told me about them in the first place. I needed answers, even though she gave me the willies.

I came out through the woods and into the clearing. It didn't smell like fried fish and roasted peanuts anymore. It smelled like animal doo-doo.

A bunch of men with no shirts on loaded steel beams and big bales of wire fence into trucks. Some of the horses from the merry-go-round were lying down sideways. They looked funny like that, like they were sleeping with their bright eyes open. Peanut shells blew along the empty lot, swirling up into the air.

I walked over to where Mrs. Snuff's tent was. Nothing was left but the four wooden stakes. I was too late.

"Hey, boy."

I turned around. It was the ring-game man, the one with the eye patch. Half his dang ear was chewed off. I hadn't seen that the first time. I wondered how in the world that could happen to somebody. It just made him even creepier.

"Yes sir?"

"What you doing? Who you looking for?"

I didn't need to tell this man my business. But Mama Frances said I had to be respectful to grownups.

"I'm looking for Mrs. Snuff," I said. "The fortuneteller lady."

He nodded his head and took a step closer. "You mean Miss Addy? What you want with her?"

I didn't like him standing this close. *None of your dang beeswax,* I wanted to say, but didn't.

"She wanted me to do something," I said, "and I need to talk to her."

I guessed that wasn't a lie.

The man didn't say anything, just looked me up and down and then spit on the ground. "Mm-hmm," he said, smirking, like he didn't believe me.

"Hey, Luke!"

The eye-patch man turned around. A white man was coming our way, wiping his hands on a dirty rag. "We need to get them horses loaded. What you waiting on, boy?"

He turned back to me and shook his head. "She lives out by the mill house, where they cut down trees. You know where that is? It's a little red shack."

I nodded. "Thank you, sir," I said, and turned to leave.

"Hold up."

I froze.

"You Curtis Hatcher's boy?"

I turned around slowly. *What if this man was somebody my daddy wronged?* "Yes sir," I said. "He was my daddy."

He nodded. "You got his look about you."

People were always saying that. Aunt Jelly said I was the spittin' image of him. That didn't make no sense. What did spittin' have to do with an image, which was another word for a picture? I turned back around and headed into the woods.

I knew where the mill house was. Cousin Zeke worked there one summer. He used to bring me pieces of wood and the two of us would whittle. Sometimes, we wouldn't talk for hours. We'd just be whittling away until the sun went down.

The trees were crowded tight in this part of the woods and the sun was blocked by all the thick branches and leaves. After a while, I came out to a clearing where the ground was red clay as far as I could see. Somebody said it was red from the blood of all the slaves that died working the land. I thought that was a sad thing.

The smell of honeysuckle rose on the air. I smelled chimney smoke, too, and passed a small rusted shack where a family called the Greens lived. Mama Frances said they were so poor their children didn't have shoes. I'd seen them around before, but never at the schoolhouse. They ran around in their bare feet, whooping and hollering. I passed coops full of squawking chickens pecking at the dry dirt, people drawing water from a well, and one place where Mr. Green slept in the weeds with a moonshine bottle lying next to him. He looked as old as Methuselah. Methuselah was a man from the Bible who was almost a thousand years old, if you didn't know.

As I walked, I wondered who the Stranger was and where he came from. I kept hearing the crow's words in my head: *A demon . . . If you don't stop him, he'll bring terror and darkness on your people.* I tried to shake off the heebie-jeebies but they stuck to me like pine needles.

The sun was still high and bright, and gnats swarmed around my head. The closer I got to the swamp, the worse the gnats got. My cousin Zeke told me one time that gnats and skeeters liked any place there was standing water.

My shoes made a *squelch, squelch* sound as I walked down a little bank and almost got sucked off my feet from the red mud. Blackbirds screamed in the trees and the deep songs of bull toads echoed in my ears. Big, fat bees were out too, buzzing in lazy circles. Little insects and butterflies were everywhere. One plant stood out from the others. I knew it was poison ivy because I got some all over my legs one time. When Mama Frances saw what happened, she mashed some herbs in a pot with a little milk and rubbed it all over my body.

Something jumped into my path. My heart rattled in my

chest. *Just an old bull toad,* I thought, relieved. Things got quiet right then. The bees stopped their buzzing. Even the wind seemed to die down. I heard myself breathing. A dog howled in the distance—a long wail that made my skin crawl. Something didn't feel right. A splash in the water made me jerk my head around, and right there in front of me, a man rose up out of the swamp.

It was the same man I saw in my dreams.

The same man I saw at Miss Carter's store.

The same man the crow told me was a demon.

The Stranger.

A black hat sat on top of his head, and his eyes glowed red. Swamp grass and green slime dripped from his clothes. "Come here, boy," he called. "Give it to me."

He reached out a long arm. A black snake coiled around it, a split tongue flicking out of its mouth.

A cold chill went right through me. I shook my head and backed up. *This wasn't real. It was all in my head. It was like the dream I had the other night, but it was in the daytime, while I was still awake. Mama Frances said one time that people could dream even if they weren't sleeping.*

"Go away!" I shouted. "You ain't real."

And then the man laughed, and it sounded like dead leaves blowing across a dusty road.

"Don't you know who I am, boy?" he called. He wasn't moving any closer. He just stood there in the swamp with the mucky water around his feet. "They call me the Stranger," he said. "I'm the sword in the lamb's belly. But you can call me Scratch. Or Crooked. You know my number, boy? It's six six six, full of tricks."

I backed up another step. I didn't like what he was saying. This was evil stuff from the Book of Revelation in the Bible. Mama Frances told me about it: the Beast and the Lamb and the Seven Seals. It was all about the end times.

And then I heard a voice inside my head, whispering. *I saw your daddy, boy. He owes me a debt, and I come to collect.*

Something sour rose up in my throat. The back of my neck got cold. *The Stranger was talking without moving his mouth! But I could hear it in my head!*

"Come with me," he said, "and I'll show you how to use that evil inside you to grow up strong." He jabbed himself in the chest with a crooked finger. "Like *me.* You'd like that now, wouldn't you? *Hoodoo?*"

He knew my name!

My heart pumped in my chest. It was beating too fast. I had to get away, but my feet were stuck to the ground. I didn't want no parts of being mixed up in my daddy's business. *Why'd he have to go and put a curse on somebody!*

The Stranger smiled, but he didn't have any teeth, just a mouth full of black, oozing swamp water. I could smell it from where I stood. His mouth creaked open like a puppet I saw at the fair one time, and he started singing.

I sold my soul to the devil, and my heart
done turned to stone.

I sold my soul to the devil; he won't let me alone.

I live down in the valley, five hundred steps.

Sold it to the devil, and my heart done
turned to . . . eeeviiilll!

My knees shook. My head felt like an apple hanging on a weak branch. The Stranger started walking toward me, the sound of his feet making squishy sounds in the water. The gnats buzzed all around me but I couldn't wave them off. *Somebody help me!* I shouted in my head, but my mouth wouldn't open. He was getting closer and his song went right through my bones.

I sold my soul to the devil; he won't let me alone.

He stopped singing and just stood there. Flies swarmed around his head. He lifted his arm and pointed a finger at me. "Mandragore," he said. "The One That Did the Deed."

"Caw! Caw!" A great shadow swooped down and blocked out the sun. Giant wings flapped and beat about the Stranger's head. "Run, Hoodoo!" the old crow called. "Run, child!"

The Stranger waved his arms in the air, but that old black crow pecked him all around the head. His hat flew off, and instead of hair, a nest of snakes sprung up from his scalp, squirming and hissing. The crow kept pecking the Stranger's head, flapping its wings in his face, squawking and shrieking.

"Run, boy!" it cried again. "Run like the wind!"

I tried to move. I felt the sweat beading up on my forehead. Pain shot through my arms and legs.

"No!" I shouted, and with all the strength I had, I lifted my leg.

I could move again!

And that's when I took off like a bolt of lightning.

Tree branches whipped out and scratched my face, but I kept running.

My legs burned and my heart pounded in my chest, but I kept running.

I tripped on a tree stump and a bunch of beetles scurried out, but still, I kept running.

I ran and ran and ran, until finally, a little red shack by the mill house rose up in the distance.

NINE

Pow-Wows

I bent down and rested my hands on my knees. They were trembling. Sweat ran down my face like I'd just come out of the swimming hole. I took big gulps of air, trying to get my breath back.

Give it to me, he'd said. Give him what? I didn't have nothing of his! I just had my old pillowcase bag, and it was empty.

I saw your daddy, boy. He owes me a debt, and I come to collect.

What did my daddy do?

I turned around to make sure the Stranger wasn't on my tail, then let out one more big breath and knocked on the door of the little red shack.

One Mississippi . . .

Two Mississippi . . .

Three Mississippi . . .

I counted to five, but nobody came. I knocked again, louder this time. "Mrs. Snuff!" I shouted.

No answer.

I waited another minute, turning around every few seconds to look at the path that led out of the woods. I thought I'd see a tall, black shape come slinking into the clearing any second.

Mandragore. The One That Did the Deed.

I wiped my forehead with my hand. Sweat still slicked my face. Something sharp pinched my foot. I looked down. I was so caught up, I didn't even realize I'd lost a shoe when I was trying to get away.

I knew better than to go into somebody's house when they weren't there, but I also knew Mrs. Snuff might have some answers about all this craziness. There was no two ways about it. I took a deep breath, turned the handle, and stepped inside.

The one-room shack was small and cramped and smelled like herbs, old tobacco smoke, and who knew what else. A rocking chair sat in the middle of the room, still rocking, like somebody just got up out of it.

It was dark inside, but a little sun shined through one dirty window. A black cat lay curled on a ratty old couch, its yellow eyes blinking. "Ain't afraid of no old black cat," I said. But I think I said it out loud to make me not so scared. It didn't work. The cat watched me cross the room, hair rising off its back in little spikes.

All kinds of tangled roots and leaves hung on pieces of rope from the low wooden ceiling. There were things on shelves too, lined up in mason jars: frogs and little lizards, the dried skin of a snake, a possum tail, blue and red powders as fine as sand, and in one jar, what looked like a tiny human skull, but I never got close enough to really see.

"Mrs. Snuff?" I called again, this time a little more quiet. I knew I shouldn't be in here. Mama Frances would whup my behind if she ever found out. But there had to be something here that would help. I had to find out what Mrs. Snuff knew about me and the crow and the crossroads and the Stranger.

I walked over to a little altar she had set up, just like the one at our house. A bowl of water sat next to some red candles with wax dripping down them and onto the table. What looked like plain old dirt was in another bowl, and some kind of half-burned, funny-smelling tree branch was there too, along with some playing cards. I picked up a few. They were bigger than the cards Aunt Jelly and I used to play hearts. One of them had a man hanging upside down, another one showed an angel blowing a trumpet—that must've been the angel Gabriel, I figured—and another showed a skeleton riding a black horse, holding up a sickle. A sickle is a long, curved knife for chopping down crops, if you didn't know. I got the shakes right then and dropped the cards back on the table.

Next to the table was a big tree stump with some stuff set on it. The top of it was smooth, like somebody had sanded it down. The Holy Bible was sitting right on it. I was afraid to touch it. *Jesus was watching me. I knew He was. This was a sign*

I wasn't supposed to be in here. Next to the Bible was another book. I picked it up. A picture of an owl was on the front.

POW-WOWS
or
LONG LOST FRIEND

A Collection of Mysterious & Invaluable Arts & Remedies for Man as Well as Animals

I didn't understand what that meant. I flipped it open. The words on the pages were small and hard to figure out. I could read pretty good at the schoolhouse, but there were some big words in there I'd never seen before. I turned a page.

Shivers ran up and down my spine.

Somebody had drawn a chopped-off hand, with long, nasty fingernails.

I took a deep breath. Underneath the hand, in big black letters, it said:

MAIN DE GLOIRE

I swallowed.

I didn't want to look — didn't want to know nothing about it — but I read down the page, sounding out the words:

> Let all who seek know the power of the talisman.
> Mandragore, derived from the mandrake root, a
> corruption of the French *Main de Gloire*, which
> is to say "the Hand of Glory."

That was it. That's what the Stranger was looking for. But what did it have to do with me? I let out a breath and kept reading:

Take Heed!

The Hand of Glory is the left hand of a man hanged from the gallows. If the man did do murder, it is known as the Hand That Did the Deed, the deed being murder!

Beware!

The more wicked his crime, the more powerful his hand!

I stopped reading. My throat felt like I had a chicken egg in it. I squeezed my eyes shut but then opened them again. I had to keep reading. I had to know why the Stranger was after me.

Listen! For Here Is Wisdom.

Beware! He who holds the Hand of Glory may use the dead man's fingers as candlewicks, which cast an unholy light, by which the dead can be called from the grave to do the owner's ghastly work, spreading death and destruction in his name.

My mouth went dry. I tried to lick my lips but it felt like cotton was in my throat. I stuffed the book in my pillowcase bag. And then someone opened the door.

TEN

Mrs. Snuff

Mrs. Snuff stood in the doorway.

One hand rested on an old knobby walking stick, and the other held a straw basket filled with a bunch of weeds and roots. She was stooped and bent over and even smaller than I remembered. Her dress looked like a potato sack. That cloudy eye of hers roamed over me. I knew I was in a whole heap of trouble.

"About time you came to see me, boy," she finally said.

I told her everything.

Meeting the crow, seeing the Stranger at Miss Carter's store and down at the swamp, the dreams. She listened the whole time, just looking at me with that milky eye of hers. I thought she was going to put a spell on me and turn me into a toad, but she didn't. After I was done, she sat back in her chair and rocked back and forth for a real long time. I fidgeted in my seat, not knowing what to do.

"Why's this demon after you, boy?" she finally asked.

I shivered. Even though I'd seen the Stranger in my dreams and down at the swamp, to hear her call him that made it real.

"I don't know," I said. "I thought you might know. That's why I . . . why I came to see you."

She didn't answer but just kept rocking in her chair, back and forth, back and forth, creaking the whole time. She was so small she looked like a little child.

She closed her eyes. "I've been feeling his presence in the town," she whispered, "like a black shadow creeping across the sun." She reached in one of her pockets and took out an old balled-up hankie and snorted into it. "When you saw that stranger in the swamp, you were in the spirit world. That was his shade you saw. Did you know that?"

"No ma'am," I said. "What's a shade?"

"His shadow self."

I didn't know what that was either.

"See, boy," she went on, "I believe this demon has the power to travel in the land of spirits. You do, too — that's why you been seeing him."

"Me? Traveling in the spirit world?"

"Yup," Mrs. Snuff croaked. "And that old crow, too. It saw you were in danger. Even though you were in the otherworld, that stranger still could've harmed you. I think that crow was drawn to you because of your deep magick."

You got some magick in you, but I think it's buried. Way down deep. That's what Mama Frances said.

"I can't do magick," I said. "I've tried before, but nothing ever happens."

Mrs. Snuff raised her head up high. I got a creepy feeling when she stared at me with that eye because I couldn't tell where it was looking. "We'll see about that," she said. "Don't make no sense for a boy named Hoodoo . . . to not know hoo-doo."

I figured she might be right about that.

"Let me see your hands, child."

I remembered the last time she wanted to see my hands. Her old claw pinched my skin. But I didn't have much choice. I came to see her, and here she was, as simple as that.

I stood up and put my hands out in front of her. She leaned forward in her chair and took them in hers. Her fingers were dry, like old twigs. She pointed to a long line that made a curve in my left palm. "That's your lifeline, right there." She jabbed it with a crooked yellow nail.

"Ow!" I cried, but she just ignored me.

"But see," she went on, "it got cut short . . . right here."

I looked at the line. It stopped in the center of my hand. "Why'd it get cut short?"

Mrs. Snuff chewed her lips. "Now, that I don't know, Hoodoo. Old Mrs. Snuff don't know everything. Some things she can see, and some she just can't. They're like pictures that come when they want to. Understand?"

"I think so," I said.

She reached up and took my chin in her hand, then turned my head one way and then the other. I felt her eyes roaming over my birthmark. "Your people say anything to you about this mark?"

"No ma'am."

"Hmpf," she said, letting go of my chin. "Gotta have heart. Bring me that bag over there." She pointed to a burlap bag on the floor by the couch. The cat watched me the whole time, yellow eyes gleaming. The bag wasn't heavy, but I felt something inside of it. I handed it to Mrs. Snuff and she reached inside. Whatever it was she took out was nasty-looking—all wrinkly and gray.

"Aha," she croaked, seeing my face. "Ain't nothing to be afraid of. This here chicken foot will get rid of the bad juju left from that demon."

I didn't know what bad juju was, but figured it wasn't good if it had to be gotten rid of. I got the willies right quick. "It's okay, Hoodoo," she said.

She took my left arm in her bony hands and started chanting, scratching me with the chicken foot the whole time. It didn't hurt, but it felt kind of funny, like somebody was tickling me. She did the same thing to my other arm, the words coming fast and quick. I didn't understand them at all. Maybe it was African. That's where Mama Frances said hoodoo came from. But she also said it came from all over the world, so I wasn't sure.

After Mrs. Snuff was done, my arms felt all prickly, like I'd been rolling around in the grass.

She put the chicken foot on the table. I didn't want to look at it.

"Now, one more thing," she said. "You need a talisman to keep away evil."

I didn't know what that was and my face must've shown it.

"It's something you wear or hold in your hand. Something that will protect you, like a mojo bag."

"My Mama Frances made a mojo bag for me one time," I said, "but it didn't work."

Mrs. Snuff winked at me. "That's 'cause you got to believe, boy."

I sighed. Everybody kept telling me that.

"What you need is a cat's-eye stone, a piece of broken chain, and a rat bone." She reached back in the bag and pulled out a red cloth sack with a piece of rope around it. She handed it to me. "Put them in this here bag, and then spell it and keep it with you at all times. You hear?"

"Yes ma'am," I said, but wondered how I was going to spell the bag when I didn't know how to conjure. "Thank you . . . Mrs. Snuff."

"You just call me Addy, boy. That's my Christian name."

"Yes ma'am," I answered, but still didn't call her Addy. That just didn't seem right.

"Now you get yourself home before your people have a fit."

I headed for the door.

"And keep that mojo bag close, you hear? That's a powwow. Don't let nobody else touch it. Keep it in your pocket."

"Yes ma'am," I said again.

I reached for the door handle.

"Hoodoo?"

I turned around. "Yes ma'am?"

"You forget something?"

She picked up my pillowcase bag from the floor and held it out in front of her.

Dang! That bag had her book in it. The one I stole. She *was* gonna turn me into a toad.

"C'mon, boy," she said. "I ain't got any more time for your foolishness."

I eased out a breath and walked the few steps to take the bag. She smiled a sly grin. "You bring that book back when you're finished with it, too," she said.

"I didn't mean to—"

She narrowed her eyes. At first I thought she was going to scold me for stealing, but if she wanted to do that she would've already done it, seeing as how I broke into her house.

"I think you might be needing it," she said.

"Thank you, ma'am," I said.

Mrs. Snuff raised her hand and tapped a finger to the side of her head. "A wise man don't look for danger," she said, "but he'll die for a cause he knows is righteous."

"What does that mean?"

She smiled. "That's for you to figure out, ain't it?"

She winked at me with her good eye before I turned the handle and stepped outside.

ELEVEN

A Broke-Down Shack

"Boy, where in God's name have you been?"

Mama Frances rose out of her chair.

The kitchen was dark, except for the glow of the kerosene lantern. I didn't feel a chicken egg in my throat anymore. Now it was a goose egg.

I lowered my eyes. "Just around," I said. "I was out collecting stuff."

She shook her head. "You and your dang collecting. If you stay out this late again I'm gonna whup your narrow behind." She paused and cocked her head to the side. "Matter of fact, go get me a switch right now. And don't come back with no small one, either!"

I gulped.

"I'm sorry, Mama Frances. It won't happen again. Promise."
I tried to smile. That usually worked.

"Sweet Jesus," she said, shaking her head again. "Just get yourself up those steps before I change my mind. And don't even think about supper!"

That was fine with me. I wasn't hungry anyway.

I felt bad because I was telling a lie. But what could I do? I didn't want my family getting hurt. Their fate was in my hands, like Mrs. Snuff had said.

Before I went to sleep, I lit a candle and put it on the table beside my bed. I didn't light it most nights because the moonlight came through the window and helped me sleep. But tonight, there was no moon, and the room was so dark I couldn't see my hand in front of my face.

After everything I'd seen today, I decided to say my prayers out loud instead of inside my head. I knelt at the foot of the bed and put my hands together like a little steeple.

"Dear Jesus, please protect me and my family. Mama Frances, Pa Manuel, Aunt Jelly, and Cousin Zeke. Oh, and Bunny, too. Please shine Your light on us and protect us from evil. And send that stranger back to hel—I mean, protect us from the man called the Stranger. And please tell my mama hello, too. Thank You, Lord. In Jesus's name. Amen."

I climbed into bed and pulled the quilt up around my neck. I'd put Mrs. Snuff's powwow book in Daddy's trunk and the mojo bag under my pillow. She'd said to keep it close, and I didn't want Mama Frances finding it. She'd have all kinds of questions, and I had to do this on my own. That's what Pa Manuel told me once. "Hoodoo," he'd said. "Sometimes you gotta take things into your own hands."

That's what I was doing—taking things into my own hands.

Hands.

The Hand of Glory.

The *Main de Gloire.*

I blew out the candle and started counting my numbers.

Bunny sat with her back up against the pecan tree in our yard, whittling a stick with her pocketknife.

It was morning, and the sun felt good on my arms and neck. I'd never seen a girl whittle before, but it looked like Bunny'd done it a thousand times. A little pile of wood shavings fell in the lap of her skirt. I'd told her all about how I found Mrs. Snuff and what I had to do.

"You saw him?" she said, her mouth wide open. "The . . . Stranger?"

She stopped whittling and folded up her knife.

"Yeah," I said. "But Mrs. Snuff said I saw him in the dream world. She called it his shade."

Bunny's face soured. "I would've gone with you. We could fight that old stranger together!"

"I have to do it on my own," I said. "Remember what I told you? I don't want nobody getting hurt? That stranger is after *me,* and I have to stop him. It's my business."

I felt like a grownup all of a sudden.

Bunny smiled. She opened up her knife and started whittling again. "You set your mind to it, you can do anything, Hoodoo. That's what my mama always says."

"You know where to get a cat's-eye stone?" I asked her.

She bit her lip. "Ozzie has a ring with a cat's-eye. I'll see if he can lend it to me."

"I don't know if I'll be able to give it back," I said. "Mrs. Snuff said I need it for a mojo bag to keep away evil. I need a rat bone, too."

"I bet we can find one of those," she said. "You can come by tomorrow, and then we'll look for a rat bone. We can have some lemonade, too."

"Okay," I said, then leaned back up against the tree. Sunlight came down through the leaves and warmed my face. Bunny set down her knife, closed her eyes, and whistled a little song.

After a minute, a woodpecker started rat-a-tat-tatting on a tree trunk. We sat there for a long time, not saying a word, just listening to the bird pecking holes in the wood. Finally, some big old cicada bugs swooped down from the trees and started clacking all around us. We both jumped up and took off running. Bunny was laughing and screaming as she ran, swatting at her head the whole time. Let me tell you, it was the most fun I'd had in a while.

Later on, after Bunny had gone back home, Mama Frances fried up some chicken livers in a black iron skillet. Usually I liked liver and grits, but I wasn't hungry. She sat across the table from me and watched me fiddle with my food. She reached out and put her hand on my forehead. "You feel warm, boy."

"I'm okay," I answered.

"Mm-hmm," she said. "You sit right there a minute."

She got up and opened a tin sitting by the stove, then took out some little jars and boxes and set them down. Next, she put some milk on the coal stove and lit the fire. She started humming.

"What you doing, Mama Frances?"

"You just sit tight. Gonna make something to help that fever pass."

After the milk was hot, she poured it into a cup and then mixed in some of the stuff she took out of the box. A funny smell rose up in the air, like something burning. She walked over and set the cup down in front of me. I thought about that elixir Aunt Jelly had made a while back. I hoped this one wasn't as strong.

"You go ahead and drink that, baby," she said. "Then carry yourself upstairs to bed."

I lowered my head and sniffed it. "What's in it?"

Mama Frances blew out a breath and leaned back a little. "That's just some dog fennel. It'll do you right, boy."

I'd never heard of dog fennel, but I figured Mama Frances knew what she was doing, so I picked it up and drank it down. It didn't taste too bad—kind of plain, like I was sucking on some leaves. She watched me drink it all, and when I set down the cup, put her hand on my forehead again. "You go on upstairs, Hoodoo. Close your eyes and count your numbers."

I headed up the steps.

The next thing I knew, I was flying.

A flattened penny sparkled in the sun. I was looking down at the railroad tracks from way up above.

I smelled wildflowers and heard dragonflies buzzing in the air, saw fields of sugar cane and white bulbs of cotton.

It felt real. Maybe I was in the spirit world. Mrs. Snuff said I could travel in the land of spirits. I wasn't sure I wanted to, but it looked like I was.

The last thing I remembered was Mama Frances making me that drink and then counting my numbers.

But now here I was.

Somewhere.

Black shapes moved behind my eyelids, like smoke and swirling water. I felt a pull, like the wind wanted me to go a certain direction. I followed it—past tall treetops and birds' nests, over little rivers and swamps, above soot-stained chimneys and yards with dogs and children running in circles. I could see it all. I was flying!

And then I smelled something bad.

Like that time a possum got stuck under our house and died. The smell was coming from a little broke-down shack. It was a pitiful place, with tall weeds, a twisted fence, and an old truck tire in the front. Burned, black tree branches made a little hill where someone had once lit a fire. And then I saw a bunch of things inside my head all at the same time: a hole in the ground with fire shooting out of it, a goat with yellow eyes, and a swarm of flies as big as a cloud.

Hoodoo?

I knew that voice. It was Mrs. Snuff's. She must've been in the spirit world too.

What you doing, boy?

I don't know. Am I dreaming?

You flyin', child, like all our people used to.

The Stranger. I gotta find him.

I felt Mrs. Snuff sigh, like wind across my face.

You ain't ready for that, boy. Now go back to your body. Just think about home and your Mama Frances. And your little lady friend. Bunny?

I didn't want to go back. I felt powerful. I was flying. I could do anything!

Hoodoo? *Her voice was like a whisper tickling my brain.* Listen.

But I didn't.

I felt cool air on my face. A black shadow was over my head. I flinched and looked up. It was the crow. Careful, Hoodoo, *the crow squawked.* Bad juju here.

Mrs. Snuff's voice had gone quiet. Maybe I'd shut it out of my mind, but I wasn't sure. The crow flapped its wings and I followed it, down to where it settled on the wooden slats of the porch. Caw! Caw! *it cried, bobbing its midnight-black head in the direction of a splintered door. I thought about what Mama Frances said, that the crow could be a trickster. But it helped me the last time I saw the Stranger. Maybe it would again. I took a breath and felt myself pass through the door.*

I couldn't see my arms or legs or any part of my body, but it felt like I was really there, inside that shack. Things were a little fuzzy, like I was looking through a dirty mirror. The room was cold, and ashes glowed in the fireplace. I felt myself settle, like I'd just swooped down from the air and landed on my feet.

I looked around the room. This was the Stranger's house. I knew it. I could feel him, just like Mrs. Snuff could.

I've been feeling his presence in the town, like a black shadow creeping across the sun.

And then I heard it. Something I'd hoped I'd never hear again:

I sold my soul to the devil; he won't let me alone.

That was his song. The Stranger's. It floated all around the room, but I didn't see him.

I live down in the valley, five hundred steps.

Something moved at the corner of my eye. I turned.

A black shape flowed down the chimney like molasses and oozed on the floor. I blinked, and a second later, it rose up into the shape of a man.

I see you, boy.

The Stranger shot out of the fireplace with a roar, flames licking all around him. His feet looked like a goat's, split in two. Red coals burned where his eyes should've been. My heart pounded in my chest. I could feel it even though I couldn't see myself. The Stranger turned his head left, then right, nostrils sniffing the air.

Think you're brave, boy? Show yourself. Give me that hand! Mandragore!

Even though I didn't have a body, I stayed still, barely breathing. The demon turned his ugly neck back and forth, snorting and sniffing. And then I felt his eyes pass right over me.

He couldn't see me!

I heard Mrs. Snuff's voice coming from far away, floating through the heavy air. Come back to your body, child! I said you ain't strong enough!

But I remembered something else she said:

Don't make no sense for a boy named Hoodoo . . . to not know hoodoo.

I'm not afraid of you! *I shouted at the demon, balling my left hand into a fist. It was tingling like a swarm of angry bees.*

The Stranger turned his head.

Hoodoo! *Mrs. Snuff cried.* No!

And that's when the demon stretched out his arm. It was too long, like a piece of black licorice, stretching and stretching.

And then he touched me.

Freezing cold went right through me, like I'd just put my hand in an icebox.

The Stranger yanked at my left hand, like he was trying to pull it out of its socket. Sharp nails scraped my invisible skin. I heard the crow screaming, but I couldn't see it.

Gimme that hand, boy! *the demon cried.*

I tried to pull away, but he wouldn't let go. The Stranger's mouth opened, and it was way too big, like the mouth of a cave, as black as a moonless night.

Nooooo! I screamed.

And then there was darkness.

TWELVE

From Darkness to Light

I floated in a black space without a body.

It was cold, but I didn't have arms to hug myself. If I could've shivered inside my invisible skin, I would've.

I tried to move but couldn't. The only thing that made me know I was still me was my thoughts, just floating . . . floating . . .

Slowly, it all came back to me. I was flying in the spirit world. I had seen him. The Stranger. And I'd heard the crow. And Mrs. Snuff, too. She tried to warn me.

The force of a thunderbolt clapped inside my head.

I felt a pull, like something yanking at me. I heard voices and saw shapes, but everything was foggy, like looking at a reflection in a scum-covered pond.

"Hoodoo!"

A voice!

"HOODOO!"

I woke up. Mama Frances leaned over me.

"What happened?" I asked. I was in my room. On the darn floor. My mouth was as dry as old hay, and my bones hurt.

Mama Frances helped me up to the edge of the bed. "You screamed," she said. "What have you been doing, child?"

I had to think quick. "It was a dream," I lied. "One of those nightmares."

"You see that crow again?"

"No ma'am."

She let out a long sigh and sat down on the bed. Then she looked dead at me. "I want you to tell me what's happening, Hoodoo. I know you think you're grown, but you ain't. If there's trouble, me and your Pa Manuel need to know about it."

I tried to look away, but her eyes locked on me and wouldn't let go.

"I'm going to ask you again," she said. "What have you gotten yourself into?"

I stared at the floor. A little moonlight came in through the window and made her face shine. An owl hooted and I almost jumped. "I'm okay," I said. "Promise."

Mama Frances shook her head back and forth and then rose off the bed. "Child, there are things in this world you don't know nothing about. Terrible things. We need to know you're safe."

I gulped.

"You stay right there a minute. I need to do something."

She left the room. I heard the floor creaking as she walked downstairs.

Was I doing the right thing? What would she say if I told her about flying in the spirit world, seeing Mrs. Snuff, and everything else?

I was thinking hard on that when I heard heavy footsteps and the door swung back open. Mama Frances was carrying a pail of water. She set it on the floor. "Hold still," she said. She knelt down a little and groaned, like it hurt. My feet dangled off the bed. She picked up my left foot, then cupped her hand and poured some water over it. She did the same thing with the other one, saying some prayers the whole time.

"The Lord watches over you, Hoodoo," she said. "He is the shade at your right hand."

Mama Frances's hands felt good, holding my feet like that, spilling the water over them. Jesus washed His disciples' feet. He did it to show humility. Humility is showing people you don't think you're better than them, if you didn't know.

I closed my eyes. Mama Frances started singing a church song, one that I knew well:

Yes, we'll gather at the river,

the beautiful, the beautiful river.

Gather with the saints at the river

that flows by the throne of God.

She started humming then, in the same rhythm as the song. I wanted to stay right there, safe with Mama Frances. I had to protect her. Her fate was in my hands.

Why did the Stranger want my hand?

I didn't have a whole lot of time to think about it, because the next thing I knew, it was morning and birds were singing outside my window.

THIRTEEN

Rat Bone

I didn't wake up on my own like I usually did. Mama Frances had to come upstairs and shake me. She made me drink three glasses of water and watched while I did it. She also gave me some more of that dog potion. I remembered she'd washed my feet before I went to sleep.

The whole while I walked to Bunny's, I thought about what happened yesterday. I couldn't get that picture of the Stranger out of my head. *I see you, boy.* And then he oozed out of the fireplace, all black and slimy.

Think you're brave, boy? Show yourself. Give me that hand!

"Hoodoo?"

"Hoodoo?"

"Huh?"

Bunny looked at me like I was crazy. "I asked if you were hungry."

We were at her house, sitting on the couch, but not too close together. It smelled like lemons and peppermint candy. There was nice furniture and a rug on the floor, too. Pictures of Jesus hung on the walls, along with one of Bunny's mama and daddy in their church clothes.

I wiped some sweat off my head. I didn't want to wipe it on her furniture, so I balled my hand into a fist and then didn't know what to do with it. I just wanted to get that cat's-eye stone and a rat bone.

"No," I said. "Mama Frances made me Cream of Wheat before I left."

"I like grits better," she said.

I was about to tell her that I did too, but her mama came walking out from the kitchen. I smelled her perfume all the way across the room. It made me think of fresh rain and strawberries.

"Hoodoo Hatcher," she said, hands on hips. "I haven't seen you all summer. Now, how've you been doing?"

I swallowed. "Hi, Miss Viola," I said. "I'm fine."

"Good, good," she said. "And how's Miss Frances?"

"She's fine, ma'am."

"Well, you tell her I said hello. Okay?"

"Yes ma'am."

Miss Viola stood there a second, looking at the both of us. Then she shook her head, gave a little smile, and walked back into the kitchen. I guess she thought we were cute or something. Bunny turned to me and rolled her eyes.

Just when I was about to ask Bunny about Ozzie's ring, her mother came back in, carrying something on a plate. "Got some fresh lemonade right here," she said, setting two tall glasses down on the low table in front of us. "It's Bunny's favorite. Isn't it, baby?"

Bunny reached for her glass. "Yes ma'am," she said. "It's sweet."

"Just like you, baby girl."

Bunny rolled her eyes again. Her mother tilted her head sideways. *"Girl,"* she said. I thought Bunny was about to get in trouble for giving some sass, but then her mama started laughing, and Bunny laughed along with her. They were just messing with each other.

Miss Viola wasn't as serious as Mama Frances. She was more like Aunt Jelly, with her pretty clothes and painted lips. Her face lit up in a smile. "When you finish that lemonade, you both can have one peppermint candy."

Bunny eyed the glass-covered dish on the table.

"Just one," her mother said.

"Yes ma'am," we both answered at the same time.

"Now, you two have fun," she said. "Don't go running off too far, you hear?"

"Yes ma'am," we both said again.

She went back through the kitchen. Me and Bunny picked up our glasses at the same time. She raised her glass in the air.

"What do you want to toast to?" she asked.

"Toast?"

"That's when you wish on something and touch glasses. Raise yours up."

I raised my glass so it was right next to hers.

"Here's to putting evil back in its place," she said.

I figured that was a good one, so we clinked our glasses together and then both took a sip. I sucked my lips. Bunny's mama was right. It was the sweetest lemonade I'd ever tasted.

Bunny looked toward the kitchen and then turned back to me. She took something out of her pocket—a handkerchief with flowers stitched on it. "Ozzie said you could keep it," she whispered. "I told him all about your troubles, and he said he wanted to help."

She took the ring out of the hankie and handed it to me. I guess they called it a cat's-eye because that's exactly what it looked like. The stone was gold like honey, and a white line ran right down the middle. A silver band held it in place.

"You sure he said it's okay?" I asked. I couldn't see how somebody would just give away a ring this pretty.

"Yup," she said. "Ozzie has all kinds of stuff. He's what you call a businessman. C'mon. Let's go outside."

I drank the last of my lemonade, and Bunny grabbed two peppermint candies from the glass dish. She handed me one, and I stuck it in my pocket for later.

Outside, she took out her knife. "Use this," she said, handing it to me.

I unfolded it and then started digging at the stone. After a minute or two, it popped out and landed at my feet. I picked it up. The sun made it shine and sparkle.

"Now we need to find a rat bone," she said. "Right?"

"Right," I answered. "One rat bone."

I already had the broken piece of chain. I'd collected it a long time ago, when I found that bird skull. Maybe I somehow knew I was gonna need it one day. *Was that fate?* I wasn't sure.

We walked around to the back of Bunny's house. There was a bunch of junk spread out in the yard: an old wheelbarrow turned on its side, a truck tire with flowers growing out of it, and a rusted outhouse in the tall weeds. The ground was muddy from the rain a few days ago, and I got some on my shoes. That made me think about my backside at the carnival, and I felt foolish all over again.

We searched around in the grass and the damp dirt by the outhouse, even walking farther out and into the cotton field. I saw a dead rabbit, but that just wouldn't do.

"What's this?" Bunny said, looking down.

It was a dead rat, lying on its side, under some dried-out cotton bulbs, little feet curled up to its body, like it was praying.

"How am I gonna get the bone out?" I asked her.

Bunny looked at the rat. "Well, like my daddy said, there's only one way to skin a cat."

"Or a rat," I said.

Skinning a rat was the last thing I wanted to do. I didn't even know how.

"Well," Bunny said, "first we gotta cut it down the middle."

I gulped. She said it like it was nothing—like she was asking me if I wanted more lemonade or something. I thought about the dead hog I saw that time with my cousin Zeke.

I swallowed, took a deep breath, and looked down at the rat. Two long teeth stuck out of its mouth.

"Go 'head, Hoodoo."

"Well," I said, "it's already dead. Not like I'm gonna hurt it. Right?"

"Right."

I knelt down and nudged the rat with a stick shaped like a fork.

Now, I'm not gonna tell you everything I did right then because you might get sick, but I did it with my eyes half closed, the knife making squishy sounds as I cut through the soft skin. It was kind of like that time I saw Zeke skinning a squirrel. To tell you the truth, it wasn't as bad as I thought it'd be.

Bunny moved in closer, leaning over my shoulder. Her pigtails were loose, and her hair brushed the side of my face. That made me more nervous than the dang rat. "Looks like all you gotta do now is pull out the bone," she said.

I didn't say anything. I was concentrating and didn't want to mess things up. I let out a breath and pulled on a little leg bone until it popped out, nice and easy-like.

We walked back to her yard. Bunny's family had a well, and she used a bucket on a chain to draw up some water. We didn't want to put the rat bone in the bucket, so Bunny cupped her hands and poured some water over the bone while I held it. That got off the rest of the blood and gunk.

I cleaned off the knife and gave it back to her. I was proud of myself.

"See that, Hoodoo?" she said, folding up her knife. "You did it."

She was right. I did do it. Without even getting the jitters.

Now I had what I needed to make that mojo bag.

Bunny turned up her nose and sniffed the air. It smelled like her mama was frying up some fatback. Fatback is like bacon, if you didn't know. Mama Frances always put it in her collard greens.

Bunny eased the bucket back down the well. "Guess we should get back," she said.

"What's that?" I asked, pointing at the ground by her feet.

She knelt down on one knee and picked it up. I moved a little closer to get a better look. She stood up and handed it to me. I turned it over in my fingers. It was white and picked clean. "Looks like a rat bone to me," I said.

"Well," she said, "my kitty does kill a lot of rats. Guess we should've looked around a little more first."

She giggled. "Oh, Hoodoo. That is something else. All that work skinning a rat, and here's a bone ready for the taking."

I shook my head. That was dang foolish. But Bunny started laughing, and the more she laughed, the more I did too, until we were both laughing our heads off.

But then I started thinking about what else I had to do.

Mrs. Snuff said I had to spell the bag. That meant I had to open that powwow book.

The one I stole.

The one with a picture of a chopped-off hand.

FOURTEEN

Jump Back, Evil

The next day I stayed close to home. I was tired, and every now and then got a headache on both temples. Maybe flying in the spirit world had some consequence. I learned that word in school: *consequence*. It was something that happened because of something else, if you didn't know. Like if you ate a bunch of Squirrel Nut Zippers on the way home and then weren't hungry for supper, that'd be a consequence.

Mama Frances cooked up some fried green tomatoes in the afternoon and I ate a couple slices. She always put hot pepper juice on hers, but the one time I did, it felt like my tongue was on fire.

I loved watching her cook. She knew right where everything was. I bet she could cook with her eyes closed if she wanted to. She must've thought I was doing okay and not worrying about nothing, but she didn't really know what was going on. I had to put a spell on a mojo bag to keep the Stranger away. I knew she would've helped if I'd asked, but I didn't want to. I had to do it myself. I had to believe.

Don't make no sense for a boy named Hoodoo . . . to not know hoodoo.

After I got done eating, I went up to my room and pulled the powwow book from Daddy's trunk.

POW-WOWS
or
LONG LOST FRIEND

A Collection of Mysterious & Invaluable Arts & Remedies for Man as Well as Animals

I didn't want to look at that drawing of the Hand of Glory

again, so I flipped past it. There were spells to stop bleeding, dry up warts, get rid of a toothache, cure a snakebite, and all kinds of other problems.

I didn't even know what I was looking for until I saw it:

AGAINST EVIL SPIRITS AND ALL MANNER OF WITCHCRAFT:

Prayer to Saint Michael

Maybe this was what I needed to spell the mojo bag. The Stranger was an evil spirit, and I was going against him. Saint Michael fought against the devil in heaven, if you didn't know.

The words were written in Bible talk. I needed to say them like I believed them. That's what everybody kept saying, so that's what I did.

Saint Michael the Archangel, defend me in battle.

Be my defense against the wickedness and snares of the devil.

May God rebuke him, I humbly pray, and do thou,

O Prince of the heavenly hosts, by the power of God,

thrust into hell Satan, and all the evil spirits,

who prowl about the world seeking the ruin of souls.

Amen.

The room was already quiet, but I swear it got even quieter. I could hear myself breathing.

I flipped through more pages. A picture of a little sack, like the one Mrs. Snuff gave me, was drawn on the page. At the top, it said:

FIXIN' A HAND:

Jump Back, Evil

A *hand* was another word for a mojo bag. That's what folks around here called them. And "jump back, evil" sounded about right. That's what I wanted to happen: I wanted evil to jump on back. I kept reading:

Rat bone
Cat's-eye stone
Broken link of chain
Salt
Candles
Saint Michael prayer and card
Kananga Water
John the Conqueror Root

I didn't know who John the Conqueror was, but I liked the way those words sounded. And what kind of water was Kananga?

I already had most of this stuff, but I needed to get the other things, too. If I went by Aunt Jelly's, she might have a picture of Saint Michael, but I didn't have time for that. She'd probably make me do some dang chores before I could get out of there.

I put the book down and thought real hard. There was only one place where I could get that picture.

I went into Mama Frances's room and started snooping around. If she came up the stairs, I'd hear her. She was too old for sneaking.

A big old cedar chest was pushed up against the foot of her bed. When I was little, I used to climb inside and close the top. Me and Bunny took turns getting in, and whoever stayed in the longest won. Thinking about that now gave me the willies.

I opened the lid. The smell of roses, perfume, and mothballs came drifting up in my nostrils. Mama Frances used to have some old Bibles in here along with a few church fans, but all I saw was old clothes and quilts, so I closed it.

I walked over to what she called her vanity—a big wooden table with a bunch of stuff on it. There was some pocket change, a few pieces of jewelry, and the Holy Bible next to a vase of dried flowers.

I picked up the Bible. It was old, and the blue cover was about to fall off. Little pieces of paper stuck up between the pages. She must've marked where her favorite psalms were. I flipped to the back to the Book of Revelation. Sure enough, there was a picture of Saint Michael. His foot was on the neck of the devil. Big white wings came out of his back like a bird's, and his shining sword was raised up high. I liked Saint Michael. If anyone could protect me, I knew he could.

I still needed that John the Conqueror Root and the funny-sounding water. I could get the salt and the candles easy enough, but what about the other stuff? I couldn't go back to Mrs. Snuff's. She'd already helped me enough.

And then it hit me. I knew just where to find the rest of those things.

I tucked the Bible under my arm and crept out, thinking hard about how I was gonna make evil jump back.

FIFTEEN

It Lies Hidden

The cowbell rang when I stepped into Miss Carter's.

Mama Frances was already gone to clean people's houses when I woke up, so I didn't have to make up any stories about where I was going. I just hoped Cousin Zeke would be working.

But he wasn't.

"That Miss Frances's boy?"

I gulped.

The blind man stood behind the counter wearing his dark glasses. I couldn't see his eyes. I didn't even know his name. One time I heard somebody call him Jooba—or was it Jubba? I couldn't remember which, so I didn't say either.

"Yes sir," I said. "I came to sweep up in the back."

I didn't like lying, but I had to. It was just a white lie. That's what Aunt Jelly called them.

"Okay, Hoodoo," he said. "Broom's over there in the corner."
He pointed a long brown finger. "Bring out one of those boxes
of cane syrup when you finish. It's called Steen's. If you don't
know how to read, there's a picture of a house on the front."

"Yes sir," I said. "I can read."

"Good," he said. "Do your book reading and grow up smart."

He went back to work behind the counter, picking up stuff
and moving it to different shelves. He was big but walked real
smooth. His shoes squeaked on the floor.

I picked up the broom and stepped into the back. I closed
the door behind me.

It wouldn't be right if I didn't do any sweeping up, so I did
that first. After a few minutes, I had a whole bunch of dust balls
in each corner. I swept them all together and then emptied them
into a metal bucket.

Now I could do what I came to do.

I knew folks came in here to get their conjure potions, but I
didn't know where they were kept. Boxes of candy were on the
shelves, and bigger boxes were stacked up on pieces of wood.
The room was small, with one high window that let in a little
sun. Every few minutes I heard the cowbell out front clang-a-
lang, and then people talking and laughing.

I looked at the shelves. Maybe what I needed was behind
the boxes of candy. They went back a few rows deep, so I moved
a couple of them out of the way to find out. I sighed. There was
nothing behind them but white painted bricks.

I pushed the boxes back into place. One of them slid too far and pushed a brick about three inches in, like there was room behind it.

I smiled inside. Those bricks were loose.

I looked to the door. I hoped Jooba—or Jubba—didn't come in here all of a sudden. I turned back to the shelf and started pulling out bricks. One by one, I lifted them out and put them to the side. When I moved the last one, my mouth fell open.

Small bags, bottles, and boxes were all crammed in there together. The first thing I pulled out was a box with a picture of a lady with red lips on the front. "Love Potion," it said. I didn't need no love potion. Another bag said "Angelica Root" and another read "Five-Finger Grass."

I heard voices again and looked to the door, but nobody came in. I turned back to the wall and started rooting around. There was all kinds of stuff in there: Hot Foot Powder, Gambler's Luck, Law Keep-Away, Anointing Oil, a bunch of different-colored candles, little bottles of liquid with no name on the front, and a bag with a drawing of some roots on it. I picked it up. *John the Conqueror Root!*

I stuck it in my pocket.

Next, I looked at the bottles. Most of them were brown and I couldn't see inside them. I shook one with no label and heard liquid sloshing around. I set it down. Another said "Uncrossing Oil." I didn't know what that was. I reached for a clear green bottle with a long neck. Some flowers were on the front, along with the words "Kananga Water" in long pretty letters, like a lady would write. I didn't know how much I needed, and I couldn't just pour some in my pocket, so I took the whole bottle.

The door opened a crack.

I froze.

"You done in there, Hoodoo?" the blind man called. "You making dirt or cleaning it?"

"I'm coming right now," I said.

The door closed shut.

I let out a big breath and pushed the bricks back into place, then stacked up the candy. I took one last look. Everything was just the way I found it.

I headed for the door but then stopped. I'd almost forgot: Steen's syrup. I'd tasted that syrup before. It was thick and sweet, like molasses.

I turned around and looked at the big boxes on the wooden slats. My eyes roamed over the words printed in black letters. There it was, off to the side, with a picture of a house on the front. I picked it up, carried it to the door, and pushed it open.

A man with a straw hat sat on an apple crate near the front counter, plucking on a guitar. It didn't sound very good and was all jangly-wangly.

Jooba or Jubba looked up. "You clean up good back there, boy?"

"Yes sir," I said, setting the syrup on the counter.

"You find what you were looking for?"

Gulp.

"I was just cleaning," I said, walking toward the door.

"Hey, Hoodoo."

I turned around, my hand just an inch from the doorknob.

"Don't you want no candy?"

I bit my lip. I couldn't take any candy. That just wouldn't be right.

"No sir," I said. "I'm okay."

He nodded his head. "You tell your Mama Frances I said hello, okay?"

"Yes sir."

Outside, I wiped the sweat off my head and ran home, my pockets full of stuff to make evil jump back.

SIXTEEN

Conjure

Night birds called outside my window.

I turned in the bed, trying to get to sleep. I kept thinking about those things I took from Miss Carter's.

I stole.

That was wrong. I had to make it up somehow, when I was done with all this.

I turned on my side. I'd already tried counting numbers and it didn't work. I said a little prayer and that made me think of something else, so I whispered it out loud:

Saint Michael the Archangel, defend me in battle.

Be my defense against the wickedness and snares of the devil.

May God rebuke him, I humbly pray, and do thou,

O Prince of the heavenly hosts, by the power of God,

thrust into hell Satan, and all the evil spirits,

who prowl about the world seeking the ruin of souls.

Amen.

I breathed out slowly. I couldn't believe I knew the whole thing. That meant something. It had to. Maybe Saint Michael was already looking out for me.

After supper that night, Mama Frances went outside to get some mason jars from under the porch. She said she was going to make a pie for tomorrow: a peach one, my favorite. When I thought about that, I felt bad, seeing as how I was doing all this sneaking.

I put the things from Miss Carter's in my pillowcase bag and went downstairs.

Mama Frances came in, brushing dirt off her hands. Her eyes traveled from my face to the pillowcase bag and then back up. "Where you think you're going, child?"

Please don't make me open this bag, Mama Frances. Please.

"I was gonna go collect some stuff."

She came all the way into the kitchen and stood real close. "If you come in this door after dark, Hoodoo, you may as well bring the switch with you. Understand?"

"Yes ma'am," I said, and stepped for the door.

"Hoodoo?" she said.

I froze. "Yes ma'am?"

"You remember what I said the other day?"

I thought about that. I didn't have an answer, so I scratched my head.

Mama Frances sighed. "I said you need to come to me or your Pa Manuel if you see anything strange, didn't I?"

"Yes ma'am," I said.

She stared at me. "If I find out you've been keeping something from me, you won't be able to sit for a week. I promise you that. You hear me?"

"Yes ma'am," I said for the fourth time.

I could feel her shaking her head at me as I walked out the door, even though I couldn't see her.

I walked to Bunny's house real slow. I was thinking about what I had to do. The powwow book and all the other stuff I needed was in my bag. I wanted to spell it on my own, but since Bunny helped me find the rat bone and cat's-eye stone, I figured I had to let her come along.

The whole time I was walking, I was thinking about the Stranger. I kept my eyes peeled. I didn't think he'd try to get me in the middle of town, but that didn't stop me from looking back every few seconds.

By the time I picked up Bunny and we got to the Cliff, sweat was running down my back. We found a place to sit, and I took out the powwow book and flipped it open. "Look," I said, pointing to the picture of the Hand of Glory. "That's it. That's what the Stranger's looking for. The Hand That Did the Deed."

Bunny's lips moved as she read over the words. "If the man did do murder, it is known as the Hand That Did the Deed, the deed being murder."

She looked back up and stared at me. "What's that got to do with you, Hoodoo?"

"I don't know," I said.

We sat in silence for a minute. A hot breeze sighed through the trees. "That stranger said he wanted my hand," I finally said.

Bunny's eyes grew wide. "He must be the one who cut off those people's hands at the graveyard!"

A shock went right through me.

Think you're brave, boy? Show yourself. Give me that hand!

I shivered. I hadn't even thought about that. I remembered that scream floating on the air: *Lord, Jesus!* It seemed like a long time ago.

"Well," Bunny said, "if he comes anywhere near us, I'll chop *his* fool head off!" She reached in her back pocket and flipped out her knife.

I had to laugh at that, even though I had the creeps.

A tree root jabbed my backside, so we got up and moved to another spot. I took all the stuff out of the bag, stuck the candles down in the dirt, and lit them with a match. Bunny watched me the whole time.

An owl hooted and I jumped inside my skin.

I took out the Bible and turned to the page with Saint Michael, then pressed in the center so it was lying down flat. The candles, the Bible, and all the other stuff made me think about the altar Mama Frances had at home. I took the red pouch out of my bag.

"What you gonna do now?" asked Bunny.

"I gotta put in this here John the Conqueror Root."

I opened the pack and reached inside. The root was brown and scratchy-feeling, and about the size of a small rock. I took out a piece and put it in the mojo bag.

"Hoodoo?"

"Uh-huh?"

"Where'd you get that stuff?"

I swallowed hard. I could've said I got it from Mama Frances, but that'd just be telling lies on top of lies. "Miss Carter's," I said. "I had to take it, Bunny. I'm gonna pay for it when I get done with all this."

She nodded. "I believe you," she said.

I looked inside the mojo bag: cat's-eye stone, broken chain, rat bone. I'd almost forgotten one last thing. I reached in my pocket and took out the pinch of salt I put there earlier and sprinkled that in too.

"There," I said. "Now we gotta pray over it."

I opened up the powwow book. Bunny moved one of the candles closer and put a rock on the pages to keep it open. I was pretty sure I could remember the prayer without looking, though.

"Hold hands," I said.

She gave me a little smile, then reached out her hand. I took it in mine. I felt like a grownup because I wasn't shy about it. This was serious business.

We sat real still. The candle flame waved back and forth. After a minute, when I didn't hear nothing but my own heartbeat, and with Saint Michael looking on, I closed my eyes and said the words. I didn't even open them to look at the book.

Saint Michael the Archangel, defend me in battle.

Be my defense against the wickedness and snares of the devil.

May God rebuke him, I humbly pray, and do thou,

O Prince of the heavenly hosts, by the power of God,

thrust into hell Satan, and all the evil spirits,

who prowl about the world seeking the ruin of souls.

Amen.

I swear it got so quiet right then you could hear a fly walking on a piece of cotton.

"You okay, Bunny?" I asked.

"I'm okay," she said. "You okay?"

"Yeah."

My left hand tingled. It was hot, like I was holding it too close to a flame. There was a sharp smell in the air too, like right before a lightning storm.

"There," I said. "Now I gotta spit in it."

Bunny screwed up her face. I felt right foolish doing it, but went ahead and spit in the bag.

"That's what you call fixin' it," I told her, and pulled the little string tight.

"Open that bottle, Bunny."

She picked up the Kananga Water and unscrewed the top, then handed it to me. I poured a little into my palm and then rubbed it on the bag. "This is called dressing the mojo bag."

Bunny looked at me like I knew my stuff. *I was doing hoodoo!*

I took the bag and waved it over the flame, making sure it didn't pass through it. That's what the powwow book said to do.

"That's it," I said. "Now we're done."

I stuck the bag in my pocket.

We sat there for a few more minutes, not saying anything. The sun was just starting to set and hung low and orange in the trees. The air was cool on my face. Every now and then I heard a splash in the river. Did fish sleep, I wondered, or were they always swimming?

I needed to get back home. I didn't want to get a switch so Mama Frances could beat my butt. That didn't make no kind of sense: getting a switch to beat your *own* behind with.

"Hoodoo?" Bunny asked.

"Yeah?"

"You got to be careful."

"I know," I said. "Mrs. Snuff said I'm supposed to keep this mojo bag close."

"Good," she said. "Now that stranger won't be able to get to you."

I wondered about that, and hoped it was true.

SEVENTEEN

The Man with Two Faces

I was gonna get my butt beat.

It wasn't all the way dark yet, so we ran as fast as we could. I knew the paths through the woods like the back of my hand, but I still tripped on some big tree roots and landed with my face in the dirt. My elbow got banged, too.

By the time I got Bunny home and then made it to my own house, sweat slicked my face. Now it was really dark. *Dang!*

If you come in this door after dark, Hoodoo, you may as well bring the switch with you.

I opened the door real quiet-like. I just knew Mama Frances was gonna be up waiting for me. I crept into the house on my tiptoes.

Cousin Zeke and my granddaddy sat at the table, looking all serious. *What was Pa Manuel doing here?* The only time he

came over was to chop firewood or drop off big bags of potatoes. Were they gonna take *turns* beating my behind?

I was in trouble.

"Sit down, Hoodoo," my granddaddy said.

I walked a few short steps and pulled out a chair. It scraped
the floor, as loud as thunder. The lantern on the table glowed
dull yellow. A moth flew around it, banging into the light over
and over. Nobody seemed to care enough to shoo it away.

I looked at my granddaddy, dressed up in a suit and a tie
like always. His skin was as light as a white man's, and his wavy
hair lay flat on his head. He had a mustache that curled up on
both ends, like a cowboy's I saw in a schoolbook. Some folks
said his daddy was a slave master who got one of the slaves to
have a baby. Whenever I asked why Pa Manuel looked like a
white man, people told me to let sleeping dogs lie. I didn't know
what that meant, and when I asked Mama Frances, she said it
meant to keep my fool mouth shut.

"Hey, Hoodoo," Zeke said, kind of soft-like.

"Hey, cousin," I said.

Mama Frances came in from the kitchen with a glass of sweet
tea. She put it down beside Pa Manuel. There was a bad feeling
in the air, like two cats circling each other just before they got to
spitting and hissing. I didn't understand how two people could
be married for a long time once but not like each other anymore.

Pa Manuel picked up the glass and sniffed it.

Mama Frances rolled her eyes. "Emanuel Hatcher," she spit
out. "You think I'm gonna jinx you in front of this child?" She

shook her head. "Sweet Jesus." She always said this whenever she was fed up with something. *Sweet Jesus.*

I was confused. *How come Mama Frances wasn't looking at me like she was gonna beat my behind?*

My grandfather sipped slowly and then swallowed. He licked his lips and then nodded like everything was okay. Mama Frances sat down at the table and continued to shake her head.

Pa Manuel looked at me. "Your grandmama told me what's been happening with you, Hoodoo."

Dang! I knew she'd say something.

"Tell me all of it," he said, setting down his glass, "and don't leave nothing out."

I looked to Zeke and then Mama Frances. Their faces were blank. That meant I'd better tell the truth, so I started talking.

Pa Manuel listened without saying a word. His gray eyes seemed to go right through me. I told him about Mrs. Snuff at the fair, the old black crow, the nightmares, and the flying dream too. Mama Frances looked at me like I was crazy. All this time she'd been telling me to come to her, and now it was finally spilling out. I wasn't trying to keep secrets. I just wanted to keep my family safe.

When I was finished, Pa Manuel leaned back and pulled out a little cigar from inside his suit jacket. He picked up a match from the table and scratched it against the bottom of his shoe, then lit the cigar and blew out a cloud of smoke. The air suddenly smelled all sweet and syrupy. He leaned forward a little and his chair creaked. He stared hard. "Is that all, Hoodoo? Everything?"

I bit my lip. Cousin Zeke and Mama Frances were still staring at me. I blew some hot air out of my mouth and, as much as I didn't want them to, the words just kind of fell out. "I saw him," I said. "The Stranger. Down at the swamp. He wanted to chop off my hand."

"Hoodoo!" Mama Frances cried. "What've I been saying all this time? Didn't I tell you to come to us?"

"Didn't want to cause no trouble," I said. "I didn't want nobody getting hurt." I stared at my feet.

Pa Manuel looked at me and said something under his breath. His face was tight. "That's right Christian of you, Hoodoo, but this here is serious business. You should have come to me or your Mama Frances."

"Yes sir," I said.

Mama Frances shook her head back and forth. "Fool, child," she whispered.

"Why's he looking for me?" I asked. "I didn't do nothing! Why's he want to chop off my hand?" It all came out in a rush, before I had a chance to think about it.

The room went silent. Zeke coughed and took out his hankie. He wiped his forehead. That made me think about the first time I saw the Stranger, when Zeke looked like he was having a conniption.

It was getting hot, like the Stranger and his fiery breath was in the room with us.

Pa Manuel looked to Mama Frances. "There's something we got to tell you, boy," he said, "and there's no better time than now."

I swallowed hard.

He took another drink and set down the glass. "When your Mama Frances told me about you acting strange lately, I got to thinking."

My left hand felt all wet and clammy. I rubbed it with my other hand. Pa Manuel's eyebrows rose up like fuzzy caterpillars. "Your hand feeling funny, Hoodoo?"

"Yes sir—I mean . . . no."

He tilted his head. "Starting to make sense now," he whispered, combing his fingers through his wavy hair.

"Hoodoo, child," Mama Frances said. "What we got to tell you is serious. And it has to do with your daddy."

I knew Daddy was mixed up in this. I just knew it!

"What do you mean?" I asked. "He just ran off, right? That's what everybody said. That he ran off and came to a bad end."

I looked to Mama Frances, hoping she'd nod her head that I was right, but she didn't. She just sat there, wringing her hands. She looked like she wanted to come over and hug me.

"What we did," Mama Frances went on, "we did to protect you, child. We didn't want you to stumble in the world before you even had a chance to walk."

I screwed up my face. I had no idea what she was talking about.

"What does that mean?"

Mama Frances sighed. "Hoodoo, when you were little, your daddy tried to help a white man named Ernest Ford with a spot of bad luck one time. This man was a gambler, see, and meaner than two dogs fighting. He wanted something to help him win big. So your daddy made him a mojo bag that was supposed to help."

She stopped and took a hankie out of her pocket. She blew into it. Her eyes were red. She waited for what seemed like a real long time, then lowered her head and shook it from side to side.

Pa Manuel looked at her. I saw in his eyes that he still cared about Mama Frances, even though they weren't man and wife anymore.

"But supposedly the spell didn't work," Mama Frances went on, "and Ernest Ford lost a whole lot of money. I'm talking a *whole* lot of money, Hoodoo, enough to buy this little county three times over."

I sat in my chair. I didn't want to know this story. Something bad was coming. I could feel it. My hand felt itchy again.

Mama Frances sniffed. "And after he lost that money, he came after your daddy with an ax. Your daddy killed him trying to protect himself. Took Ernest Ford's ax and chopped his fool head clean off."

I shivered in my seat.

"But the man's friends said your daddy put a curse on him, and they . . . they strung him up, anyway. I'm sorry, child."

My head felt heavy, like a rock, pressing down on my neck. They never told me this. They never told me any of it. They were keeping secrets. I didn't like that one bit.

"Strung him up?" I asked.

"He was hung, Hoodoo," Zeke said. "For murder."

Something tickled my brain. Something I knew, but didn't want to think about.

"Why?" I asked, looking at all of them. "Why didn't you tell me?"

Mama Frances dried her eyes. "Like I said, baby. We were trying to protect you. No child needs to know a story like that. Not even if it's their own daddy."

No one spoke for a moment. The moth kept flying into the light, over and over and over. Pa Manuel's cigar smoke swirled in the air. "I'm afraid there's more to this here story, Hoodoo," he said.

I closed my eyes and swallowed. *What could be worse than Daddy chopping off somebody's head and getting hung for murder?*

Pa Manuel shifted in his chair. "I remember the day well," he said, looking out through the little window. "It was just getting to be dark, the day your daddy died. The sun was setting like a fiery ball in the west. It was out by the old poplar tree in Cahaba. The hangman wore a black hood with two eyeholes cut out of it, so no one could see his face."

Pa Manuel stopped and swallowed. "But not everybody was out for blood that day, Hoodoo. Some colored folks started

singing a song right then, whispering the words in the gathering
dark:

> Swing low, sweet chariot,
> Coming for to carry me home.
> Swing low, sweet chariot,
> Coming for to carry me home.
>
> I looked over Jordan, and what did I see
> Coming for to carry me home?
> A band of angels coming after me,
> Coming for to carry me home."

My eyes started stinging when Pa Manuel whispered those
words. I could see it in my head: the fiery setting sun, the hangman's hood, the poplar tree with its twisted branches. Cousin
Zeke and Mama Frances dropped their heads a little.

"They threw the noose around your daddy's neck," Pa
Manuel went on. "And that's when he started chanting. His lips
moved and whispered words I could barely hear. But I know
when a spell is being weaved, and that's what your daddy was
doing. He was conjurin'.

"And when they finally drew the rope up high and let him
drop, I saw—" Pa Manuel stopped and whipped out a hankie
from his suit pocket. He looked at Mama Frances and she nodded. Pa Manuel wiped his forehead. "I saw your face, boy. I saw
your face flash across your daddy's. Back and forth, like he was
wearing two faces."

My legs felt weak and my head went dizzy. My hand started to ache — my left hand.

I sat frozen. Pa Manuel slumped back in his chair. Mama Frances rose up and walked to a little table by the kitchen. She opened a drawer and came back with a bottle of moonshine. Pa Manuel took it and poured some in the glass he'd been drinking tea from. Mama Frances pulled out a chair closer to me and sat down again.

"Why?" I asked. "Why was my face on Daddy's?"

Mama Frances put her hand on my shoulder. "Hoodoo, at the exact moment he died, even though you were being watched by Bunny's mama at their house, you fainted and went into a fit. Bunny's mama said your eyes rolled back in your head and you couldn't speak."

I felt like the whole world had just crashed down on me. "Why?" I asked. "Why'd I go into a fit?"

Mama Frances closed her eyes a moment and opened them again. "We think your daddy was trying to do something to save his spirit."

"Save his spirit?"

Pa Manuel looked straight at me. "I believe when your daddy died, he was trying to leave his body, boy. Trying to hide his soul somewhere."

I knew what was coming. But I didn't want to think about it.

"He tried to go into *your* body, Hoodoo," Pa Manuel said. "He called on the powers of the dark, but it didn't work."

I got the shivers all up and down my arms. *He owes me a debt, and I come to collect.*

"And the force of that spell was so strong," Mama Frances said, "it stripped away whatever little magick you might've had. And we think only a *part* of his spirit went into you."

"What part?" I asked. "What part of him went into me?"

I knew the answer, but waited for it anyway.

Pa Manuel leaned forward. "Mandragore," he said. "That's what that stranger's looking for. The left hand of a man hanged for murder."

I swallowed.

"That hand you got isn't yours, Hoodoo," Pa Manuel said. "It's your daddy's."

EIGHTEEN

Stranglehold

I looked at my left hand. I balled it into a fist and then opened it again.

It wasn't my hand. It was Daddy's hand. The left hand of a man hung from the gallows. The Hand That Did the Deed:

Murder.

Pa Manuel mopped his forehead with his hankie again.

"It's called soul traveling," he said. "Something our people don't mess with, but your daddy did that day." He looked at me hard. "It's the same thing you did with your flying dream."

"I didn't know I was doing it," I said. "It just happened."

"Nothing just happens," Zeke said.

"That was some dark magick your daddy did that day," Mama Frances said. "And something was called up from the blackest night when he did it."

I shivered, and counted to five. *Maybe I was dreaming.* But when I opened them back up, everybody was still sitting in the dark dining room. "The Stranger," I said.

"I'm afraid so, Hoodoo," Pa Manuel said. "Now he's been roaming the land ever since. I reckon he wants that hand because your daddy was a powerful mojo man."

The more wicked his crime, the more powerful his hand.

"That makes the hand stronger, see," Pa Manuel said. "If the Stranger gets it, he'll have the power to call up —"

"That's enough!" Mama Frances cried, shooting up out of her chair. "You gonna scare this poor child half to death!"

"Hoodoo's not a child anymore," Pa Manuel said calmly. He fixed his eyes on me. "He needs to understand the power of the dark and the light."

I felt something stir in me at that second. It started in my belly and rose up to the top of my head, like pins and needles pricking my skin. Mama Frances took the bottle from Pa Manuel, turned it up, and took a long swallow. It was the first time I'd ever seen her drink. She sat back down and shook her head.

"My daddy brought the Stranger here?" I asked.

Pa Manuel nodded once.

"The family blood is strong," Mama Frances said. "And sometimes the sins of the father are cast onto the child."

"It's in your hands now, Hoodoo," Zeke said.

They all looked at me right then, like I was a grownup. I looked down at my hand. The Hand of Glory. *Main de Gloire.* Daddy's hand.

The room was silent. A little moonlight came in through the window. The lantern on the table burned low.

"You got to face your evil, Hoodoo," Zeke said. "If people don't face the danger that's seeking them, evil will find them first."

I looked at him, and then Mama Frances, and then Pa Manuel.

They had no right! They'd been telling lies and keeping secrets all this time. They thought I was too much of a baby to know about my daddy.

We sat there until the lantern burned all the way down, not saying a word. The moth fluttered around a few more times, and finally folded its little wings and didn't move again.

I cried in bed, and when sleep finally came, bad dreams came with it: the hangman's hood with flames burning in the eyeholes, creeping things that slithered on the ground, and the words to that song Pa Manuel whispered floating on a hot breeze.

Swing low, sweet chariot,

Coming for to carry me home.

When I woke up, my head was foggy, like smoke was swirling around on the inside. Downstairs, Mama Frances was in the kitchen cooking up something, like always. She didn't say good morning, just gave me a small smile and tipped some grits onto my plate. I had a headache and rubbed my head with two fingers.

"I know that was a lot for you to hear last night, Hoodoo," she said. "About your daddy."

I didn't answer. I just stirred my grits. I wasn't hungry.

"But you have to know the truth, sometimes," she said. "Even though it's painful."

"Yes ma'am," I said, staring at my plate.

Mama Frances came and sat down next to me. She reached out to touch my hand, but I drew it back. She cocked her head, but didn't look like she was gonna scold me. *How could she be mad at me after they were the ones keeping secrets all this time?*

"You got to be extra careful from here on out," she said. "Your Pa Manuel is going to help you."

"Don't need no help," I said. "You said the sins of the father are cast onto the child."

She narrowed her eyes. "Yes, I did say that, but—"

"Well, I'm Daddy's son," I said, still looking down at my plate. "I have to take care of this myself."

Mama Frances's eyes sparkled a little. "Like I said, Hoodoo. We kept this from you because you weren't old enough to know. We were trying to protect you."

Lies. Lies. Lies. Lies.

"Uh-huh," I said. "I understand." And then I set to eating my grits.

Bunny sat on a tree stump out back, laying down cards for a game of hearts. I was in no mood for hearts but went along with it anyway. She'd come by after breakfast and I'd told her what Pa Manuel and Mama Frances had told me.

"Daddy was a coward," I said. "Nothing but an old scaredycat! How could he do that?"

Bunny gave me a sad look. "Oh, Hoodoo. I am so sorry. Maybe he *had* to do it. You know, maybe something was making him do it. I'm sure he didn't want to."

"They kept secrets," I said. "All this time. They thought I was too little to know what really happened."

My eyes started stinging all of a sudden.

"He killed a man and then they hung him! That stranger wants his left hand. And it's on me, Bunny! It's on me!"

She reached out to touch my shoulder, and the next thing I knew I was crying, right in front of her. I couldn't help it. The tears just rolled down my cheeks all salty and hot. I felt anger rising up in me like a dark cloud.

Bunny took my left hand and turned it over in hers. "I'm sorry, Hoodoo," she said.

"He knew what he was doing—trying to send his soul into mine. He was scared and didn't want to die." I yanked my hand away.

"That is a mess," she said. "A dang shame."

She dropped her head a minute and then looked back up. "Does it feel any different?" she asked. "Like it's not really a part of you?"

"No," I said, wiping away a tear. "I never noticed nothing before, except . . ."

"What?"

"It's been itching something fierce. And sometimes it gets hot or cold."

Bunny looked scared but was trying to hide it. I could tell.

"But you've got that mojo bag now," she said. "You fixed it and dressed it. That's gotta help, right?"

"I hope so," I said. But deep down inside, I knew it wasn't enough.

After Bunny left, I went walking. I needed some time to think. I thought about what Pa Manuel had said the night before—that Daddy was trying to save his spirit. It wasn't right for him to do what he did—trying to send his body into mine. *What would've happened if that spell had worked? Would I have disappeared?* That just didn't seem right.

I had to have a plan. I needed to find the Stranger before he found me.

You got to face your evil, Hoodoo, Zeke had said. *If people don't face the danger that's seeking them, evil will find them first.*

Evil wasn't gonna find me first. I was gonna find it.

I passed Miss Carter's and thought about going in to see Zeke but didn't. People were sitting outside on apple crates playing dominoes. Cigar smoke floated on the air. Maybe I could find that shack where the Stranger lived—the one I saw in the spirit world. I could rush in and . . . what? I didn't even know how to stop him.

I sat down on the little steps in front of the schoolhouse. The teacher, Mrs. Gaines, liked to make things out of old junk. She said she was an artist. One of the things she made was right off to the side in the tall weeds — a bunch of steel and wood and rope all nailed together to look like a man's face. It had bottle caps for eyes, a slat of wood for a mouth, and bent, rusty nails for hair. I didn't really understand it, but I liked looking at it. Maybe that's what art was: something you could look at to make you feel better.

"Hey, Doo-doo, what you doing, boy?"

I turned my head and stood up quickly, my left hand clenched.

J.D. Barnes and Otis Ross came out of nowhere, both of them looking up to no good. I sucked in a breath. Dirt streaked their faces like they'd been digging around in the mud. Lookin' for treasure, they called it. I didn't know what kind of treasure they expected to find around these parts.

They stepped closer. Sweat dripped down my back.

"I asked you a question," J.D. said.

"Leave me alone," I said, not looking at either of them. "I'm not bothering you."

"You got any money?" Otis spit out.

I didn't answer.

"Where's your girlfriend?" J.D. teased. "Funny Bunny. Isn't that her name?"

I raised my head and looked at J.D. He was about four inches taller than me, but it may as well have been six feet. He put his face just a couple inches from mine. He smelled like he hadn't had a bath in ages. "Now," he said slowly, drawing out the word, "I think you need to be taught a lesson. That fool Ozzie ain't here to help you this time."

I gulped, and faster than lightning, J.D. kicked out with his left foot and swept my legs out from under me. I went down with a crash, right on my tailbone.

"Woo-eeee!" Otis yelled. "Hoodoo Doo-doo afraid to fight!"

He ran in circles, like a crazy dog chasing its tail.

I pushed myself up on the heels of my hands. J.D. bounced on his toes and raised his fists.

"Get him, J.D.," Otis said.

But before J.D. had a chance to swing—before I even had a chance to think of what I was going to do—my left hand shot out and grabbed him around his neck.

And then I lifted him up.

I swear, right off the ground. His legs dangled in the air and his eyes grew as big as a bull toad's.

"Stop!" he croaked, choking out the word. "Stop!"

Otis just stood there with his mouth open like a barn door. But I didn't want to stop. I felt strong. My left hand was all pumped up with power. Now *I* was the one in charge. "You gonna pick on me again?" I asked, looking up at him.

"No!" he grunted. "Promise!"

"Better keep your fool mouth shut!" I said, just like Mama Frances always told me. I unclenched my fingers and J.D. fell to the ground like a sack of potatoes.

Otis looked like he'd been hit by a box of hammers. "That was voodoo," he said, all afraid. "No wonder they killed your daddy."

My blood boiled when he said that. My left hand was hot and cold and itching all at the same time.

I took a step toward him. "It's hoodoo," I said. "Not voodoo, stupid."

He stepped back and put both hands up in the air, like he was surrendering.

"I think you better leave," I said. "And don't come back."

Otis bent down to help J.D. "Leave me alone!" he shouted.

J.D. stood up and shot me a dirty look. He muttered something under his breath—probably some curse words—and then the both of them stomped off into the woods.

I stood there for a long time, not even moving, and then finally looked down at my left hand. I felt the blood pumping through it, throbbing in time with my heartbeat.

Right about then there was only one thing running through my mind:

The more wicked his crime, the more powerful his hand.

NINETEEN

A Storm Is Coming

I sat in the backyard under the pecan tree. My hand still felt full of power, like I could reach down and pull roots right out of the ground.

A squirrel skittered up the side of the tree and climbed into the higher branches. I heard it rustling around, and a minute later, some pecans rained down around me. I picked one up and rolled it between my fingers.

I was walking around with a dead man's hand.

I let out a breath. I felt something—a little tickle that ran along my left arm and then settled in my hand. The pecan trembled in my palm. I barely saw it shake, but I felt it. I thought about the Stranger trying to yank my hand off in the spirit world. I thought about J.D. and Otis and everyone else who ever picked on me. And then, right out of nowhere, the pecan flew out of my hand.

A bunch of leaves got caught up in a circle and rose into the air. I stood up. Tree limbs creaked and whipped back and forth. Birds flew out of the high branches, making a racket. The clothes Mama Frances had put out on the drying line flapped and snapped in the wind. Little clouds of dirt swirled around, getting into my eyes. I spit dust out of my mouth.

It's too much! I need to calm it down!

I closed my eyes. My ears were plugged up like I'd just put my head underwater. I took deep breaths. *Stop!* I said inside my head. "Stop!" I yelled out loud.

My left hand was balled up in a fist. All this time I'd been squeezing so hard, my nails cut little marks in my palm. I slowly uncurled my fingers. "Be still!" I shouted.

And the storm stopped in an instant.

I raised my left hand and looked at it. I made a fist and then opened and closed it. My breath came short and quick. One of Mama Frances's sheets was hung up in a tree, flapping in the quiet wind, like a ghost.

I looked at my hand again. *What else could I do?*

Flood the river and drown everybody in town? Call lightning from the sky and split a tree in two? My head was spinning, and I couldn't think on one thing at a time.

But then I realized what else I could do with this hand.

I could kill that dang stranger.

• • •

Mama Frances slid a hot hoecake onto my plate. Hoecakes are like flat cornmeal fried up in bacon grease, if you didn't know.

"Funny storm yesterday, huh, Hoodoo? Just rose up out of nowhere. Now, what would cause something like that to happen?"

I stared at my food. She knew. Just like always. I couldn't hide nothing from her. "I didn't know I could do it," I said. "It just kind of happened. I just thought real hard, and the wind rose up like that."

She sat down and reached across the table, placing her right hand over my left one. "That power you feel coming on isn't something to play with. You have to be careful. Understand?"

"Yes ma'am," I said, not looking at her. I was still mad at everybody for keeping secrets.

"Now eat your breakfast," she said. "You need to help me finish the washing from yesterday."

I groaned. Helping with chores wasn't my favorite thing to do. I ate my hoecakes and then went outside. Mama Frances came out of the house with a heap of clothes in her arms. "Go fetch some water, Hoodoo," she called.

We used to get our water from the well, but it was backed up and Pa Manuel needed to come over and fix it. I grabbed the bucket and headed down the path.

The stream was just a minute or two away, down a hill and under the shade of long-beard trees. The water was a silver ribbon, splashing and gurgling over smooth stones. It was always cold, even in summer. Pa Manuel said it was a natural spring, whatever that meant.

I slid down the hill, my feet planted apart sideways so I wouldn't fall. It was kind of steep, and all the dirt and red clay made a little avalanche. I learned that word at the schoolhouse: *avalanche.* That's when rocks and mud come sliding down a mountain, if you didn't know.

Could I cause an avalanche with my left hand?

When I reached the bottom, I stood on a fallen tree trunk slick with green moss. I bent down and held the bucket sideways in the stream so the water could run into it. I did this while thinking that any second I was going to see the Stranger or hear his creepy song, but by the time the bucket was full, I hadn't seen hide nor hair of him.

For a quick minute, I thought about trying to do something else with my hand. Maybe I could reach down in the stream and pluck up a catfish for supper! But I didn't think that was a good idea. Mama Frances's words came back to me: *That power you feel coming on isn't something to play with. You have to be careful.*

Getting up the hill with the full bucket was the hard part, and I almost lost half the water. When I got back, Mama Frances already had a small fire going under the black iron pot.

"Pour that water in right quick, Hoodoo," she said.

I stood up on my tiptoes and lifted the bucket as high as I

could, then balanced it on the lip of the pot and tipped it. The water hit the bottom with a loud hiss.

"Hmpf," Mama Frances said, hands on hips. "That's not a lot of water, Hoodoo. I remember a time when I used to go down to the stream and fetch two buckets myself!"

She smiled and laughed a little when she said that, and I didn't feel so mad anymore.

Mama Frances had already scrubbed the clothes with a wire brush, so she threw them in the boiling water and then added some soap called Castile. She picked up a long wooden stick propped against a tree and slowly stirred the pot. This whole thing would take a long time, because after she got done stirring, she'd have to pull the clothes out and rinse them off with clean water and then hang them up to dry.

"I'll get more water," I said, wanting to help for some reason.

Mama Frances stopped stirring and kind of leaned on the stick for a second. She wiped her forehead with her free hand. She was tired already. I could tell. I wished I had some money so I could pay somebody to work for her, like she did for other people.

I ran as quickly as I could, the bucket slapping my hip and sending a jolt up my spine. I slid down the bank and a bunch of dirt and pebbles traveled down with me, but I landed safely. I stepped into the stream, getting my shoes wet, but I didn't care. This time, I promised myself, I wouldn't spill a drop.

I heaved the bucket back up the hill, the water sloshing

back and forth. A dog was howling somewhere nearby, long and lonely.

When I got back to the yard, I saw something on the ground, right next to the big iron pot. Mama Frances must've moved some firewood. But when I got closer, I saw it wasn't firewood at all.

It was Mama Frances.

TWENTY

This Too Shall Pass

"It was a stroke," Pa Manuel said. His eyes were red-rimmed and his lips trembled.

I'd never seen a man cry before, but he looked like he was about to or had just finished. He sniffed and blew into his hankie. "Old woman pushed herself too hard," he said angrily.

I reached out to touch Mama Frances's hand. She was breathing slowly, lying in bed with a quilt wrapped around her. Her eyes were closed. She looked peaceful. I'd run to Pa Manuel's as fast as I could when I found her like that, slumped down on the ground. He told me to run back home, quick as lightning. After what seemed like forever, he finally came over with a white man named Dr. Farley, who said she was lucky to be alive at her age after a stroke.

I wiped a tear away from my cheek. I didn't want to cry.

But Mama Frances was all I had. I'd already lost my mama and daddy. I didn't want to lose her, too. I reached out with my left hand and stroked her forehead. She was burning up.

Aunt Jelly came by to look after me. I kept thinking it was my fault that Mama Frances had the stroke. "Maybe I should've stirred the clothes," I told Aunt Jelly. "That way, she wouldn't have strained herself."

She drew me into her arms. "Oh, baby, there's nothing you did wrong."

I didn't want to, but right then I started blubbering. She held me close and rubbed the back of my head. "Hush now, child," she whispered. "It's all right."

She kept saying that, but I knew it wasn't all right, and brushed the tears off my cheeks.

Bunny came by and we sat close to Mama Frances's bedside. We took turns stroking her hands and talking to her. She looked like she was just taking a nap, lying there in the bed like that. Aunt Jelly had made the quilt from some old clothes and big squares of red and yellow cloth. Rows of little houses ran along the edges, and stars were in the middle. She told me one time that in the olden days, people would put directions on the quilts and hang them in the windows so the runaway slaves would know which way to go to get to freedom.

Mama Frances wore a little mojo bag around her neck that Aunt Jelly made for healing. Candles were lit too, placed on the floor and all around the bed. Since Mama Frances couldn't talk,

I couldn't tell if she was hot or cold, so I went back and forth between tucking the quilt up to her neck and then drawing it down.

"Do you think she can dream?" I asked Bunny.

"Probably," she said. "I bet you in her dream she's walking and talking, like she used to."

Used to. Bunny's words made my eyes sting. "Will she ever get back to the way she was?" I asked. "Will she ever be . . . normal again?"

Bunny didn't answer. There was a moment of silence while we looked at Mama Frances. All I heard was her low breathing. Bunny reached over and took my left hand. "She'll be okay, Hoodoo. I know she will."

The door creaked on its hinges, and Aunt Jelly came in holding a bowl of chicken broth. She'd been trying to get Mama Frances to eat the past two days and wanted to be ready if she woke up.

I was about to get out of the way and make room for her, but she looked at me and said, "That's okay, Hoodoo. Maybe y'all being by her side will strengthen her spirit."

I turned to look at Mama Frances.

And that's when she opened her eyes.

"She woke up!" I shouted, jumping out of my chair.

"Lord above," Aunt Jelly whispered, raising a hand to her bosom. The bowl of broth crashed to the floor.

Mama Frances looked around the room like she didn't know where she was, but then her startled eyes fell on me. Aunt Jelly and I both edged closer to the bed. Bunny sat still, like she was in shock. Mama Frances's eyes were cloudy and her lips were dry. Aunt Jelly tried to give her a sip of water from the glass on the end table, but Mama Frances shook her head. "No," she groaned in a raspy breath. "I don't know how long I'll be able to speak."

We all waited. My heart felt like it was about to jump out of my chest. Mama Frances licked her lips. "It was the Stranger," she finally said. "He did this to me. You have to find him, Hoodoo. You got to destroy him!"

Aunt Jelly gasped.

"How?" I asked. "How do I do it, Mama Frances?"

She licked her lips again. "I saw our people on the other side," she said softly. "They're waiting for me, child." She raised her arm and pointed a finger in the air. "Up there."

She started coughing, and it felt like the whole bed shook. "Come here, Hoodoo. I want to tell you something."

I leaned down, and put my ear close to her mouth. I took her right hand in my left. She coughed again. "What is it, Mama Frances? What you wanna tell me?"

Her lips moved like she wanted to say something.

But she never did.

Because right about then, Mama Frances gave one last cough, and then closed her eyes.

TWENTY-ONE

From the Other Side

I cried so much I didn't think I had any tears left. It felt like the world was spinning and I was hanging on, hoping I wouldn't get thrown off and fall into darkness. Mama Frances's words echoed in my head: *It was the Stranger. He did this to me. You have to find him, Hoodoo. You got to destroy him!*

Aunt Jelly went into town and came back with some black pants and a white shirt for me to put on for the funeral. I didn't know where she got them from, but the shirt was too big and I had to roll the sleeves all the way up to my elbows. I didn't have a belt, either. I cried right then, looking down at the floor and the too-big pants rolled up to my ankles. I'd never see Mama Frances smile or hear her laugh again. I wiped my nose with the back of my hand. *I'll make that stranger pay for what he's done*, I said to myself. *I promise, Mama Frances.*

People came from far and wide to go to Mama Frances's funeral. I sat in a church pew, staring at scratches in the wood. I felt like I wasn't really there, like I was a ghost moving through the world with no place to go. I had a foggy memory of women coming up and throwing their arms around me, men shaking my hand, Preacher Wellington shouting about the reward of heaven from the pulpit, and ladies in big hats waving paper fans and crying out to the Lord. Three women in white dresses had to take people out now and then because they went into a fit.

Pa Manuel sat like a man made out of stone. I could tell he was sad, but I figured he was trying to be strong for everybody else. I guessed he still loved Mama Frances deep down inside.

By the time I went up to look at Mama Frances in the casket, I felt like I was sleepwalking. But there she was, dressed in her favorite Sunday dress. Her hat had pink and yellow flowers on it, and they'd put some paint on her lips. I didn't like that one bit. Mama Frances never painted her face. *How could she be dead?* I reached down to take her cold hand.

And a vision came up in front of me.

The Stranger crept into our yard, walking like some kind of black daddy longlegs. Mama Frances stirred the big iron pot of clothes.

"Mandragore," he hissed.

Fast as lightning, Mama Frances pulled the stick out of the pot and struck him across the head. The Stranger fell back and cursed under his breath. "Where is the boy?" he said. "The one that carries it. I come to collect."

"Leave that child be!" Mama Frances lashed out. "He's an innocent!"

The Stranger raised his left hand. Mama Frances fell back and hit the ground like she was struck by lightning. Her stick went flying. She glared at the Stranger, and her eyes were like fire. "He will destroy you, demon!" she cried out.

The Stranger's head snapped back, and for a second he looked afraid, but then he whispered a word, and it came from his thin lips in a line of black smoke, curling around his tongue.

Mama Frances shook for a second, let out a breath, and closed her eyes.

The Stranger cocked his head and stared at her. He raised his head and howled, just like a dog, then strode off with long steps until he vanished in the fields beyond the house.

"Hoodoo."

I heard a muffled voice, like it was under water.

"Hoodoo."

A hand touched my shoulder.

"We have to let her go, son."

It was Pa Manuel.

I took a deep breath, still shook up from the vision.

"Hoodoo?" he whispered, leaning in closer.

"I have to kill him," I said, staring at Mama Frances in the casket. "I don't care what it takes. He's gonna die, Pa Manuel. And I'm gonna do it."

TWENTY-TWO

Smoke and Fog

I stared at the hole in the ground where Mama Frances slept in a pine box.

Pa Manuel and Aunt Jelly threw handfuls of dirt on top of the coffin, but when it was my turn to do it, I couldn't, and let the grave dirt fall from my fingers right where I stood.

I didn't want anybody to see me crying, even though they said it was okay. Bunny tried to put her arms around me but I ran away and found a big old tree to lean against, where I hugged my knees to my chest and let the tears come.

It was the Stranger. He did this to me. You have to find him, Hoodoo. You got to destroy him!

I heard singing, coming from back in the graveyard. Preacher Wellington's voice was the strongest, deep and sad. It was one of Mama Frances's favorite songs, the one she sang when she washed my feet:

> Yes, we'll gather at the river,
>
> the beautiful, the beautiful river.
>
> Gather with the saints at the river
>
> that flows by the throne of God.

That made me cry even more.

"Damn you, Stranger!" I said, balling my left hand into a fist. I didn't care that I'd said a curse word, so I said another one. "I'm gonna send you back to hell!"

"Hoodoo?"

I looked up through my tears.

Bunny stood beside me. I was so caught up, I hadn't even heard her coming.

"C'mon, Hoodoo," she said, kneeling down. "We gotta go. Back to your house."

She took my hand to help me up.

"Ow!" she cried.

"What's wrong?" I asked.

She rubbed her fingers.

"Your hand, Hoodoo. It's hot. Like fire."

Back home, our house was jammed with all kinds of folk. Some of them weren't even at the funeral. Flowers were everywhere.

That's what happened when someone died. People brought you flowers.

I stood at the head of the dining room table. I always thought it was a lot shorter, but Pa Manuel and Cousin Zeke pulled each end and an extra slab of wood came out, making the table really long.

I stared at all the food: fried chicken and catfish, okra with corn and tomatoes, liver and onions, red beans and rice, corn bread in a black iron skillet, peach cobbler, boiled peanuts, pecan pie, yellow cake, five pitchers of sweet tea, and a big pot of chitlins (chitlins are boiled pig guts, if you didn't know). Eating was the last thing on my mind. There was a hole in my stomach I couldn't fill. I thought I was gonna be sick just looking at all of it. I kept seeing Mama Frances fall to the ground, trying to do everything she could to protect me.

It was the Stranger. He did this to me. You have to find him, Hoodoo. You got to destroy him!

I squeezed my eyes shut so I wouldn't cry again.

People kept coming up and hugging me. The ladies smelled like perfume and the men like cigars and liquor. Some of them were smiling and laughing now, once they got something to eat and some moonshine in their bellies. I felt like telling them they could all go straight to —

I needed to get away.

I pushed through the crowd. Everyone was giving me sad smiles or patting my head like a dog or something. Bunny was sitting on the other side of the room. She had a plate on her lap and was pulling apart a biscuit. She looked like she didn't even know what she was doing, like she was half asleep.

"Bunny."

She jumped like I'd scared her and then let out a breath.

"Let's go outside," I said.

It was late afternoon, and a little cooler now. We sat up against the pecan tree, not saying anything. Bunny had on a black dress and some shiny shoes. She looked different than she usually did, like she was growing up right in front of my eyes. Her eyes were damp and a little red.

I looked over to where I'd found Mama Frances on the ground. "I gotta stop him, Bunny."

She wiped her eyes with her hand. "How?"

"I don't know yet. But I will."

She didn't say anything right away—she just gave me a funny look, like a smile that didn't work right. I could tell she was trying to think of the right thing to say. She looked at the ground, then back at me, then back to the ground, but in the end, she didn't say nothing.

By the time everybody left, there was a mess in the house. Aunt Jelly gave away a lot of the food, and some church ladies helped her clean up. Somebody had stubbed out a fat cigar on one of Mama Frances's best plates. I didn't like that one bit.

I stood at the little altar Mama Frances had set up. There

were fresh flowers here too, standing up in a big glass vase. They were pretty, with green and red leaves shooting off in all directions. I sighed. Now I'd have to put something there that belonged to Mama Frances so she could watch over me. She was an ancestor now. That almost made me cry again but I sucked it up.

I looked at the other stuff on the altar. Candle flames burned bright. The ring was still there, the one with the painted eye on it. I picked it up with my left hand. It was hot to the touch. I closed my fist around it.

White light flashed in front of my eyes.

I was standing where two dirt roads met at a right angle. The crossroads. One road trailed off in the distance, where it got swallowed up in a creeping fog, rising as high as the black walnut trees. The other one was dark red clay and looked as wet as mud. I was supposed to make a choice and decide which road to take. I didn't know how I knew this. I just felt it.

It was cold out, and the sun was weak and hazy. The air felt heavy on my shoulders, like a cloak or a quilt. "Might as well go this way," I said out loud, turning and heading down the path of red clay. As I walked, my shoes didn't leave any footprints. Was I a ghost?

A white light glowed in the distance. I felt warm all over, and walked toward it, not afraid, as light as a feather. The closer I got, the more the light turned into a shape—the shape of a man.

I was only a few feet away now, and it swayed in the ghostly breeze.

"Hoodoo."

Tingles ran up and down my neck. "Daddy?" I called.

"I don't have long, son. You have to be careful."

I looked at him. I was only five when he died, and didn't remember a whole lot about him. But his face brought back some memories. I could make out his thin mustache and beard, his strong jaw, and his dark brown eyes, like two smooth stones floating in a river. I thought about the time I rode on his shoulders. "Choo, choo!" he'd shouted as we ran around the yard in circles. I squeezed my knees together and held on tight. That was one of the few things I remembered about him.

"Why'd you do it?" I asked. "Why'd you try to send your body into mine?"

The shape swirled in the breeze. "It was a mistake, Hoodoo. I panicked up there on the gallows. I wanted to save myself. I was a coward, you see, boy? I didn't have heart, like you."

I felt the soft brush of a finger on my birthmark. I was angry but didn't know what to say. He was still my daddy, no matter what he'd done.

"But what I did is unforgivable, son. That's why I'm stuck. I need my whole body to enter the kingdom of heaven. You understand?"

I nodded, even though I didn't know what he meant.

"See?" he said.

The shape raised its ghostly arm. Where Daddy's left hand should've been was just an empty stump. A bell tolled way off in the distance: three soft notes.

"How did the Stranger know you were my daddy?" I said. "How did he find out your hand was on me?"

A flash of red flickered across Daddy's ghostly face. "He troubles my dreams even in the land of the dead," he said quietly. "He probably plucked the memory of you from my thoughts, like a fishing line hooks a trout."

"They lied," I said. "All of them. Cousin Zeke, Mama Frances, and Pa Manuel. They were keeping secrets."

"They wanted to protect you, son. I caused enough pain."

The word pain echoed around me, ringing in my ears and through my body. I had so many more questions.

"But if I have your hand, why's it look normal on me?" I asked. "How come it's not a big old hand, like yours?"

"You're in the real world," he said, "and time and space are different. I guess that hand just changed to fit your body, son. I don't know."

His voice trailed off on the wind.

There was silence for a moment, and Daddy's figure waved in the air, like smoke. "Once you take care of this here . . . demon, my hand will come back to my body."

"How?" I asked. "How can I do it?"

"You will," he said. "That power you got isn't just from me. It's your strength and smarts, too. You're what they call an innocent. And the innocent can cause deeds great and powerful. You gotta use your head, son, and your heart." He touched my birthmark again.

I nodded.

164

The bell chimed once more, but this time it sounded like it was muffled by cotton, far away and close at the same time. Daddy looked past my head, like he was searching for something. I turned to see what he was looking at.

When I looked back, he was gone.

TWENTY-THREE

Knights of the Wise Men

Flash.

I stared at the ring in my palm. The candles on the altar had gone out. My head hurt and my left hand throbbed. I was dizzy, like I'd just stepped off a merry-go-round. First I'd seen what had happened to Mama Frances, and now I was seeing Daddy.

What was happening to me? Was I standing here the whole time with my eyes closed?

Daddy was trying to tell me something. This must've been his ring. I put it in my pocket and made my way on up the steps.

I needed to lie down, just for a minute. My body ached again, just like the other times I went in the spirit world. I passed the picture of my family on the wall, the one that usually gave me the shivers. Mama Frances and Pa Manuel were younger then.

Daddy stood in the sunshine with his arms crossed, right in the very front. I put my nose up against it and looked closer.

And then I saw it.

Daddy was wearing the ring.

Even though it was tiny, I could still see it, sparkling in the sun.

In my room, I took the powwow book out of the trunk and flipped through it, looking for anything that could help me defeat the Stranger. There were a bunch of drawings in the back: owls and birds and little shapes I didn't understand. I turned another page. My heart skipped.

THE ALL-SEEING EYE

The all-seeing eye is the eye of God, for
He is always watching.

It was the painted eye from Daddy's ring. Underneath the picture there were some words in the middle of the page:

FRATERNAL ORGANIZATIONS, SARDIS, ALABAMA

Freemasons Lodge

Order of the Eastern Star

Prince Hall Lodge 33

Knights of the Wise Men Lodge 1

I didn't know what it all meant, but one thing stuck out—"Wise Men."

A wise man don't look for danger, but he'll die for a cause he knows is righteous. That's what Mrs. Snuff told me.

Wise Men. Daddy's ring. It all meant something. I knew it. But what?

I flipped through the book some more but didn't see anything I thought would help, so I stuffed it back into the trunk. A piece of yellow paper was under all those things I found a long time ago: the bird skull, the flattened pennies, and the bottle caps. I moved the stuff out of the way and picked it up.

It was a picture, yellow and faded.

A whole bunch of men stood in front of a brick building, all dressed up in suits and ties. The ones standing at the edges held long sticks at their sides, with something on top that looked like a star. None of them were smiling. I shook my head. *Who were these people?*

The funny thing was, they all had on some kind of apron, like Mama Frances used to wear in the kitchen when she was cooking. But these aprons had the same symbol that was on Daddy's ring: the all-seeing eye. I swallowed hard and lowered my gaze to the bottom of the picture:

Knights of the Wise Men

Lodge 1

Sardis, Alabama, 1920

Grand Archon: Curtis Hatcher

That was Daddy!

My left hand started itching. I blinked and looked at the group of men again. Daddy was in there somewhere. All of their faces were serious and dark. Some had beards and some little mustaches. Some were fat and some were skinny, but only one of them wore a tall stovepipe hat on top of his head, just like Abraham Lincoln's: *Daddy*.

I knew it was him wearing the hat. I'd know those dark eyes anywhere. *Grand Archon*. That sounded like he was the boss. Why else would all those people be standing around with him in the middle?

I'd seen that building before, the one they were all standing in front of. It was over where Zeke showed me that strung-up hog, the one with the cut down its belly, right next to Mr. Haney's farm.

I knew what I had to do.

I had to go there.

I touched my pocket.

And keep that mojo bag close, you hear? Don't let nobody else touch it. Keep it in your pocket.

I started down the stairs. Aunt Jelly was scrubbing out pots in the kitchen. She heard my steps and turned. "Hey, Hoodoo. You should get some rest, baby. These are trying times."

I sat down for a minute. I didn't need no rest. I needed to get to that building and see what I could find. Maybe there was something in there that could help me stop the Stranger. *You gotta use your head, son, and your heart.*

"How long are you gonna stay here?" I asked her. "You can't stay here forever. You got your own house too."

The red scarf Aunt Jelly wore around her head had some sweat on it, and she didn't look her usual put-together self. "Don't worry about that, Hoodoo. I guess you'll come stay with me or your Pa Manuel."

"But what about *this* house?" I said, my voice cracking all of a sudden. "This is Mama Frances's house. We can't just leave it. It wouldn't be right!"

I didn't want our home to start looking like one of those old broke-down shacks I'd seen around the county: full of weeds and trash and stray dogs roaming around doing their business.

Aunt Jelly pulled out a chair and sat down next to me. The sweet smell of her perfume was heavy in the room. She touched my cheek and her hand was soft. "Hoodoo, you just need to sit tight. Your Pa Manuel's gonna take care of this here business."

Now *she* was telling me what to do. Everybody thought they knew what was best for me. But I was gonna show them all.

I closed my left hand into a fist.

"Now, you just settle yourself," she said. "I got some sweet tea and some hoecakes. Just like your Mama Frances used to make. Everything's gonna be okay. All right, baby?"

"I'm not a baby!" I shouted, jumping out of my chair. A pitcher of sweet tea crashed on the floor.

"Hoodoo!" Aunt Jelly cried.

I stared at her for a second and then at the glass on the floor. "I'm sorry," I said. "I have to go now, Auntie."

"Child," she said, giving me one of Mama Frances's sideways looks.

But I shot out the door before she had a chance to say anything else.

I ran.

Like if I ran hard and fast enough, I could bring Mama Frances back. But I knew that couldn't happen.

I passed Miss Carter's. A black cat sat on the tin roof, eyes gleaming like two little jewels. A dog let out a lonely bark every few seconds. The moon had come out, and some streaks of red ran through it. Mama Frances would've called that an omen.

Music was coming from a beat-up shack on the corner. The man I'd seen back at Miss Carter's a while back sat out front playing the guitar and drinking from a bottle. I heard shouting and then glass breaking through the closed door. The people inside of there were probably drunk on moonshine and who knew what else.

I kept walking, and pretty soon passed Mr. Haney's farm. Some of his chickens were running around in the dirt road, pecking at the ground. They must've gotten past his fence.

I came to a place where the road was crossed by another road at a right angle, and cut through some high grass. The building I was looking for sat on the corner. That made me scratch my head.

It's also a place where two roads cross at a right angle, and where powerful mojo can be done, but it's dangerous, because the old devil himself can sometimes rise up and cause confusion.

The crossroads.

The building was old and broke down now, with smashed windows and some trash laying around. It had an upstairs and a downstairs. Most of the bricks were dirty and more than a few of them were gone, like missing teeth. Tall, scraggly weeds grew in the front, and some smashed-up pieces of wood were stacked on the concrete steps.

I walked through the weeds. Somebody's old truck was hidden in there with the hood open and the windows smashed. I wondered why the Knights of the Wise Men didn't use this place anymore.

Right in the front, the all-seeing eye was painted on one of the bricks in blue and gold, but the colors were dull and old-looking. A little slice of moonlight shined right on it and made it glow. That had to be a sign. The powwow book said that the eye meant that God was always watching. I thought back to when I was snooping around in Mrs. Snuff's house and Mama Frances's bedroom and felt ashamed.

I blew out a breath. The air was hot, and crickets sang in the weeds. "A wise man don't look for danger," I whispered, "but he'll die for a cause he knows is righteous."

I didn't understand it then, but I did now. Righteous was doing right, if you didn't know. I learned that word at church when Preacher Wellington read from the Bible. *He leadeth me beside the still waters. He restoreth my soul: He leadeth me in the paths of righteousness.*

I looked up at the night sky. "Dear Jesus," I whispered, "if You're watching, I'm just trying to do what a wise man would do."

Two small windows were on one side of the building. I chose the one farthest away from the roads and lifted the sash. It slid up with a rusty squeal that broke the still night. I looked both ways, grabbed onto the ledge, pulled myself up, and crawled through.

I landed on a hard floor with a thud. A zing of pain shot up my elbow. I stood up and started walking—short little steps, like an old lady. Darkness surrounded me.

One step. Two steps. Three steps . . .

My toe hit something solid. I reached out and felt a smooth wooden surface, like a table of some sort. I ran my fingers across it and touched something else. It was cold and hard, like metal. I trailed my fingers up along the sides and felt something soft but kind of firm. It was a candle in a holder. I could feel the wick. I shuddered.

He who holds the Hand of Glory may use the dead man's fingers as candlewicks.

With one hand on the candle, I slowly ran my fingertips across the table, looking for matches. There had to be some. Can't have light without no matches. I didn't feel anything, so I lowered my hand down the side of the table. Most tables had drawers, I figured, so that's what I was looking for. I found one, pulled, and the drawer squeaked open, echoing in the darkness.

I spread my fingers around and felt the sharp end of a nail, some paper, and then a small box. I picked up the box, and shook it. That was the sound of matchsticks rattling around. I took one out and scratched it against the rough, pebbly side of the box.

Light surrounded me. I looked down.

It wasn't a table in front of me, but some kind of pulpit, like at church. The all-seeing eye was painted on the wood.

I wondered if God was watching me right this instant, sitting on His throne in heaven with all the angels around Him.

I held the candle up high. The floor was checked with black and white tiles, and big chairs with fancy woodwork sat at both ends of the room. Two other chairs faced each other in the middle. I walked toward the far end, holding the candle out in front of me. The feet on the big chairs looked like lions' paws.

A staircase was to my left. I walked up slowly, the old floorboards creaking under my feet. A closed door was at the top. I took a few careful steps and turned the handle. It didn't open all the way, just a little, so I gripped the candle, put my shoulder up against the wood, and pushed until the door scraped open.

The room was small and cramped and smelled like moldy rags and paint. A few broken chairs were stacked in one corner, and a small table was off to the left. On the right, a bunch of rusty keys on a big metal hoop hung from a nail in the wall. Moonlight flowed in through a window. I gazed about the place.

A human skull sat on the floor.

But I didn't get the shivers this time. "I'm done with the damn shivers," I whispered. But then I got the shivers anyway because I said a curse word.

I moved the candle closer to the skull so I could get a better look. I didn't know why I needed to do that. It was definitely a skull. There was no mistaking that. *Why would a skull be here?* But there it was, its jaw hanging open until the end of time. I reached out with my left hand to touch it but snatched it back at the last second. I imagined those teeth closing over my fingers and taking a bite.

A bunch of old books were scattered around, all covered in

dust and spider webs. I set the candle on the floor, then knelt down and started rooting through them. I didn't know what I was looking for, but I studied each cover, waiting for something that could help. I picked up each one, flipped a few pages, and then set it down on the floor next to the others. When I moved a big one aside, a black hole stared up at me. A piece of floorboard was missing and the stack of books had been covering it. I bent my head down to look inside.

A wise man don't look for danger, but he'll die for a cause he knows is righteous.

I didn't even think about it—didn't even get the heebie-jeebies—just reached in right quick with my left hand and spread my fingers around. I felt something hard. Something solid. I closed my hand around it and pulled it out.

It was another book.

A cloud of dust flew up into the air when I blew on it. A coughing fit seized my throat. I needed some water and swallowed a few times, trying to work up some spit.

The words on the cover were easy to read:

The Sixth & Seventh
BOOKS OF MOSES:
Magic, Spirits, Art

Moses was from the Bible. *Did he write this book?*

I ran my left hand across the letters, and just like that, my fingers started tingling. That meant I had to be getting close to something. I shook my wrist a few times to get the feeling back.

I let out a breath and opened the book to the first page.

What I was staring at didn't make sense. It was a drawing of a square box with a bunch of scrambled letters inside it. I scrunched up my eyes and tried to read the words.

S	A	T	O	R
A	R	E	P	O
T	E	N	E	T
O	P	E	R	A
R	O	T	A	S

Maybe it was some kind of hoodoo spell. The word SATOR was on the top and going down the left side. ROTAS was spelled on the right and along the bottom. I thought about that for a second. ROTAS was SATOR spelled backwards. My head was spinning. I didn't know what it meant. A breeze tickled my arms. The room had been hot just a minute ago, but now it was freezing cold. Someone had written their own words under the square, and I whispered them out loud.

Where he walks, it burns.

In ash, he shall be known.

Cipher and speak the Sator Square.
The evil that draws nigh is vanquished.

That didn't make no kind of sense either. The box must've been the Sator Square—I did figure out that much.

I flipped through the book and saw a bunch of pictures: there were stars, a wheel in the sky, stone tablets with squiggly marks on them, and a snake wrapped around a stick. All the other pages had tiny words crammed together, and my eyes hurt just looking at them.

A rustling sound made me jump. I whipped my head around. It was a mouse, snuffling through a pile of papers.

If I was afraid of a mouse, how could I face the Stranger?

I felt like a coward, but then Mama Frances's voice echoed in my ears:

It was the Stranger. He did this to me. You have to find him, Hoodoo. You got to destroy him!

I stood up and tucked the book under my arm. I didn't want to steal it but I knew I'd need it. There was something I had to figure out about the Sator Square.

I took the steps real slow. I didn't want to go falling through a hole like the one that book covered up. Hot wax dripped down the metal candleholder and almost burned my hand.

When I got to the first floor, I stood next to the window and blew out the candle. I set it on the floor and then pulled myself up and over.

Outside, I breathed in the fresh air, glad to be out of the

cold and dark. I got to the road the way I came in, passing the broke-down truck and all the other stuff. The moon was white and soft, glowing around the edges.

The black cat was still sitting on the roof of Miss Carter's, and watched me pass with yellow eyes. As I looked up at it, I had only one thing on my mind.

Getting back home and ciphering that Sator Square.

TWENTY-FOUR

The Sator Square

Aunt Jelly's perfume hung in the air when I got home. She must've been up waiting for me. The dishes were washed and put away and the wooden floor scrubbed clean. The table was pushed back together, making everything look normal again, like it did before all those people were here, stuffing their faces and drinking liquor.

The hoecakes Aunt Jelly had made sat on the table on a yellow plate. I picked one up and took a bite. It tasted like ashes in my mouth. I got real sad right then, thinking about Mama Frances. I'd never smell her food rising up in the morning or hear her calling me down for breakfast again.

I crept upstairs into my room. The window let in a little moonlight. I found my candle stub on the end table and lit it, then sat on the bed and took out the book.

The Sixth & Seventh
BOOKS OF MOSES:
Magic, Spirits, Art

I opened it up to the page with the Sator Square.

Where he walks, it burns.

In ash, he shall be known.

Cipher and speak the Sator Square.

The evil that draws nigh is vanquished.

I rubbed my chin. *Cipher* means to write something, if you didn't know. Mama Frances used to say that word a lot. *Make sure you go to school and learn how to cipher.* And I knew the word *nigh* meant near or close. Preacher Wellington used it in church all the time. *The time draws nigh,* he'd say, *when the Lord Jesus will return.*

But what about the other part? *Where he walks, it burns.* Who was "he" and what was the "it" that burned?

Maybe I needed to write down the words in the square first, to see if anything happened.

I reached inside the table drawer and took out my pencil and paper, the same ones I used to draw the Stranger's face before I nailed it to that tree. By the time the schoolhouse opened, I might be out of paper, I figured. "Here goes," I whispered, and started writing the letters:

SATOR

AREPO

TENET

OPERA

I had no idea what the words meant, and I had to scrunch my eyes to make sure I was spelling them right. Finally, I wrote the last word—**ROTAS**—and waited for something to happen.

One Mississippi . . .

Two Mississippi . . .

Three Mississippi . . .

The hoot of an owl broke the silence. I jumped, thinking something was about to happen, but after a few minutes, there was no sign of anything. I looked at the words in the book again.

Where he walks, it burns.

In ash, he shall be known.

Cipher and speak the Sator Square.

The evil that draws nigh is vanquished.

Cipher and speak. I'd already ciphered them. Maybe I needed to say them out loud. I blew out a breath and looked at the paper on the floor. "Sator," I whispered. The candle flame flickered in the dark room.

"Arepo," I continued. "Tenet. Opera. Rotas."

Silence.

A branch scraped the window. I imagined a long-beard tree coming to life and grabbing me off the floor with hairy arms.

I knew the words meant something. I could feel it. They crept into my head, like daggers sticking into my brain. They had something to do with defeating evil, and I needed to figure out what.

Where he walks, it burns.

Where . . . he . . . walks.
Where the Stranger walks?
But what burns? The ground?

My left hand started throbbing, like it did when I picked up J.D. in a stranglehold. I was getting close. I knew it.

Where he walks, it burns.
In ash, he shall be known.

It burns? What burns?
If you burned something, you'd get ashes. I stared at the paper.
Paper.
Where he walks, burn the paper.
Where the Stranger walks, burn the paper.

That was it! I needed to burn the paper!

I snuffed out the candle, grabbed some matches, and walked down the steps quietly. The Sator Square paper was in my right

183

hand and the candle in my left. The front door opened with a squeal and I stepped outside.

The moon was white when I left the Wise Men's club, but now it was blood-red. I saw a fat possum creep under the porch. There was no noise except for some crickets singing in the weeds. I walked around to the side of the house, right where Mama Frances had fallen.

It was the Stranger. He did this to me. You have to find him, Hoodoo. You got to destroy him!

I knew what I had to do. Now was no time to be a scaredy-cat. I lit the candle and then bent down low and waved it across the ground from left to right. It had to be here. It hadn't rained. *Where was it?*

I moved a few steps to the left and stumbled. I was in front of the big iron pot Mama Frances used to wash clothes. I lowered the candle down to the ground.

And then I saw it.

A footprint.

The Stranger's footprint.

"Where he walks, it burns," I whispered.

The footprint was big and ended in a sharp point, like a boot. I sat down in the dirt and held up the paper with the Sator Square. Moonlight passed over the letters and I read them out loud: "Sator. Arepo. Tenet. Opera. Rotas.

"Only one thing to do now," I said, and folded the paper and set it in the Stranger's footprint.

I held the candle to the paper. A yellow line of fire ran along the edge, growing brighter. I looked up at the window to Mama Frances's room. That's where Aunt Jelly was sleeping. If she saw fire or smelled smoke, she'd have a fit. But this was more important than Aunt Jelly having a fit.

The paper crumpled into ash, and wispy trails of smoke curled up and into the night sky. Wind sighed through the trees.

In ash, he will be known.

I waited, trying to breathe like normal even though I could hear the blood pumping in my ears. "C'mon," I hissed. "Do something!"

The pieces of ash started to glow.

Little sparks of red, yellow, and gold winked and flashed in the Stranger's footprint. My heart pounded in my chest. My left hand trembled. The sparks swirled in the air like a twister, then settled back down to the ground.

I leaned in, looking closer. The ash broke apart and started moving—left and right and up and down. It was making letters!

I saw a *Z* and a *C*. Then an *N*. The ash was spelling something. The letters moved in the dirt, scrambling around like a bunch of little ants. Everything else was still. Even the crickets stopped their chirping. I took a breath and looked in the footprint.

It was a name.

The Stranger's name.

The name of a demon.

I opened my mouth.

"Zacharias Cain," I whispered.

Blinding white light flashed in front of my eyes.

"Zacharias Cain! Let go of that cat!"

The black cat shrieked and twisted out of Zacharias's hands, then scampered away, a bushy tail tucked between its legs.

Zacharias looked up at his mama. His eyes were so gray, people had a hard time looking at him—sometimes, even his own mama.

"It tried to bite me," Zacharias said.

Flash.

Moonlight shone down on a circle of trees in the woods. The man called Zacharias Cain stood with a group of other men—black men and white men all standing together. Some wore fancy suits, and some wore nothing but rags. But they were all there because of Zacharias. He was the one they followed. The one they believed in.

In one hand he held a book, and in the other, a curved knife. He eyed each man in turn and then, in a voice as strong and deep as a preacher man's, read a verse from the book.

When he finished, all was quiet. The men looked at him in fear and in praise, for his voice touched them deep, deep, deep in their souls.

And when he raised his knife and stepped toward the man on the ground, they didn't look away.

When it was over, he held his blade over blue and orange flames and let the blood drip down . . . down . . . down . . .

A voice came up out of the fire. A man's voice, but different. No one heard it.

No one except Zacharias Cain.

The voice promised him great things—things beyond this world.

Flash.

Zacharias stood before a judge. Rope bound his hands, and a link of chain coiled around his feet.

"Zacharias Cain," the judge said. "You come before this court as a criminal and have been found guilty of murder."

A muscle in Zacharias's neck twitched.

"Do you have anything to say before sentencing?"

Zacharias looked up at the man and smiled.

The judge shook his head in contempt. "Zacharias Cain," he said. "I hereby sentence you to death by hanging. May God have mercy on your poor soul."

The wooden hammer came down on the desk with a bang.

As they led him away, Zacharias's gray eyes flickered. He turned to look at the man who had sentenced him to death.

"I'll see you in hell," Zacharias said.

He took the wooden steps leading up to the gallows without fear.

He had a life beyond this one, one that was promised to him by the Voice in the Flames.

He didn't hear the snapping of his neck.

He didn't see the family of the man he murdered.

All he saw was his master, who spoke to him through a cloud of flame.

Zacharias Cain would get his eternal life. But it would not be the life up above, where green things grew and the wind stirred and the birds sang.

No, Zacharias's life would be here, in this place beyond the Great Void, down in the Valley of Death, five hundred steps. He was cursed by the Great Deceiver and would walk in darkness forever.

Flash.

My ears rang. Sweat poured down my neck. I took big deep breaths and tried to calm myself. Wind snuffed out the candle. Darkness fell all around me. The pictures I saw stuck in my head. They were evil — terrible, evil things.

The Stranger was a demon *and* a murderer!

I licked my lips, cracked and dry. "I know your name," I whispered.

"Zacharias Cain, I know your name."

TWENTY-FIVE

Death Rides a Black Horse

I crept back in the house and closed the door quietly behind me. The last thing I wanted to see was Aunt Jelly coming down the steps. My head pounded like somebody was banging on my skull from the inside.

I made it to my room and lay back on the bed. I was dang tired. The whole day had been crazy. Zacharias Cain had been a murderer and now he was a demon. And Daddy had called him up from the dark.

He owes me a debt, and I come to collect.

I sat up in bed and rubbed my eyes. There was no way I could sleep.

I saw Zacharias Cain in the dream world before. Could I do it again?

I had to get to him before he got me.

I took a few deep breaths. *Concentrate,* I told myself. I let my breathing come slow and easy. My left hand felt like hot water was running over it.

You got some magick in you, but I think it's buried. Way down deep.

I closed my eyes. "Zacharias Cain," I whispered. "I know who you are. You have no power over me. I know your—"

A howling rang in my ears. I squeezed my eyes shut tighter and clapped both hands to the sides of my head, trying to block the sound. When I opened my eyes, I wasn't in my room anymore.

I was out of my body again, back in the shack where I saw the Stranger shooting out of the fireplace with flames all around him.

The room was dark, with one window and a fireplace where the embers burned low. Something moved in the corner, blacker than the black surrounding it.

It was Zacharias Cain.

He reached into his cloak and took out a bunch of things. I could see each one, even though it was dark: a lock of hair, a silk handkerchief, a pair of earrings, a shoe, a gold tooth, a knife, and a Bible. He set each one down on a low wooden table, then shuffled over to the fireplace and picked up a piece of charred wood. Just like before, I could feel myself in the room. My body was back in bed, but my mind was here. The smell of burned cinders floated in the air.

Zacharias Cain suddenly snapped his head up and sniffed, looking this way and that. I held my breath even though I knew he couldn't see me. He could feel me, just like I could feel him.

He shook his head for a second and then drew a circle on the floor with the charred wood. Inside that circle he drew a man who looked like he was part goat, sitting cross-legged in midair. Black wings unfurled behind him. Horns stood up on his head. One hand was raised with the palm thrust out, and the other with a finger pointing to the ground.

I could smell his breath here in the dream world, hot and sharp. The creature he'd drawn blazed into fire. Flames rose up and danced in the dark room. I felt myself put a hand to my face, trying to block the heat. I guessed I did the same thing back in my bed. What would happen if Aunt Jelly came in my room? Would I be lying there like I was asleep, with my eyes wide open and my hand raised to my face? If she took hold of me and shook me, would I wake up? Could I get stuck here in the spirit world?

Zacharias threw the things on the table inside the circle and then opened his arms wide, chanting the whole while. I couldn't hear the words, but I knew they were evil—they were sharp and hard-sounding, each one ending with a hiss from his lips. I shivered.

I woke with a dry mouth. I needed water. I didn't even know it was morning until I heard some birds chirping.

I sat up in bed. Something wasn't right. It took me a minute to figure it out and then I realized what it was: there was no smell of hot food rising up to greet me. Mama Frances was gone. But I didn't have time to be sad. I had to take care of business.

My left hand was throbbing. Once again, I was plumb tired. I leaned back in the bed and blew out a long breath.

You got to face your evil, Hoodoo, Zeke had said. *If people don't face the danger that's seeking them, evil will find them first.*

I jumped out of bed.

What was Zacharias Cain doing with all those things?

If someone took your things and knew the right spells, they could have power over you. Everybody who used magick knew that, even me. I thought back on what I'd seen: earrings, a shoe, some hair, a knife —

A knife.

A pocketknife, just like Bunny's.

Bunny!

I raced downstairs. Pa Manuel and Aunt Jelly sat at the table, talking quietly and drinking their coffee. I knew I was gonna get in trouble for rushing out like that the night before, but I was in too much of a hurry to stop and say sorry.

Pa Manuel turned to face me. "Hey there, Hoodoo. Hold your horses, boy."

"I gotta go. There's something I need to do."

"I'm not gonna scold you for what you did yesterday, child," Aunt Jelly said. "I understand. You were upset and these are troubled times."

"But still," Pa Manuel said. "You can't run off like that again, Hoodoo. Understand?"

"Yes sir."

He took a sip of coffee and set the tin cup on the table. "Now, listen. Me and your cousin Zeke know some men in Cahaba.

What we call hoodoo priests. Some people call them root doctors. They're gonna help us take care of this here stranger."

"Don't need no help," I said.

Pa Manuel cut his eyes at me, but I stared back at him like a grownup until Aunt Jelly leaned forward in her chair. "Now, Hoodoo," she said, wagging a finger. "You need to listen to your granddaddy. He's got a plan."

I headed for the door.

"Whoa, there," Pa Manuel said. He stood up and put his hands down on my shoulders. "What did I just say? Can't go rushing off again. You worried your poor auntie half to death last night."

Right about then I didn't care if I was gonna get my butt beat, so I let it all out. "I don't need a plan!" I shouted. "Mama Frances said I had to destroy him! I know his name, Pa Manuel! I'm gonna stop him!"

"Hoodoo," said Aunt Jelly, and her voice was sharp. "Now, listen—"

"No!" I shouted, and raced for the door.

I ran as fast as I could, down the dirt road and past the train tracks. I jumped over a wheelbarrow filled with rusty truck parts, my legs chugging and my heart racing. I heard one last shout of "Hoodoo!" from Pa Manuel, but it was far away. He couldn't run after me. He was too old for running.

My blood boiled as I ran. Zacharias Cain had taken Mama Frances from me, and he wasn't going to take no one else.

I kept running—past Miss Carter's, past the church, past the schoolhouse—but something wasn't right. It was quiet. Too quiet. Usually this time of day, there'd be people on the street, little kids running and playing in the sunshine. But not today. Today was different. Whatever it meant, it couldn't be a good sign.

I was standing in front of Bunny's house in no time. I needed to tell her what I'd seen: Zacharias Cain holding her knife.

I bent down and rested my hands on my knees, breathing hard. Sweat poured down my face. The back of my neck felt all clammy and hot. I stood up and raised my hand to knock on the door.

"Hoodoo."

I turned around quickly, my left hand clenched into a fist.

It was Bunny.

I breathed a sigh. "Hey, Bunny."

She didn't say anything for a minute, just looked at me. Her creamy brown skin was pale, and dark circles shaded her eyes. I took her hand and dropped it right quick. It was hotter than a stick of blazing wood.

"You okay, Bunny?" I asked. "You're burning up."

And this is what she said:

"I live down in the valley, five hundred steps."

"No!" I shouted, grabbing her by the shoulders. "Bunny, stop! Don't sing that song!"

"I sold my soul to the devil," she sang, and then she threw her head back and howled, and the voice that came out wasn't hers. It was Zacharias Cain's.

She slowly raised her arm and pointed beyond my head. I

turned around. A whole bunch of people from town was shuffling toward me, and they were singing a song I knew well.

I sold my soul to the devil, and my heart done
turned to stone.

I sold my soul to the devil; he won't let me alone.

I live down in the valley, five hundred steps.

Sold it to the devil, and my heart done
turned to . . . eeeviiilll!

And behind all those people, like a nightmare come to life, Zacharias Cain rode on a black horse with red eyes.

Darkness spread down the street like somebody had thrown a blanket over the sun. *How could it go dark in the middle of the morning?* Cold sweat rose up on my arms. White mist streamed from the horse's mouth.

Zacharias Cain said nothing. He just rode forward on his horse. *Clip, clop, clip, clop,* and the people sang in rhythm with the sound:

I live down in the valley, five hundred steps.

They were under his spell. I'd seen how it'd happened. He'd stolen their things and now they were his servants.

"It's him," Bunny said. "My master's here." And then she put her hand to her mouth and giggled.

I hated seeing Bunny like that, but I didn't have time to think about it. Zacharias Cain was getting closer, just taking his sweet time. My left hand was red-hot, like fire, tingling like never before.

Clip, clop, clip, clop.

Zacharias Cain reached in the folds of his black cloak and pulled something out. It was a sickle, like I'd seen on that playing card at Mrs. Snuff's, glowing in the dark that had fallen in the middle of the day. I could see how sharp the blade was from where I stood, and when he turned it sideways, it seemed to disappear.

"Mandragore," he said. "The One That Did the Deed. *Main de Gloire.*"

The sound of his voice carried all the way down the street. Now the crowd of townsfolk moved closer, eyes rolled back in their heads. They were pushing in on me, people I'd known all my life, the same people I'd seen at Mama Frances's funeral, the same people that had been at our house—but now, they were all under Zacharias Cain's spell. They chanted together, and it made my blood run cold.

O Hand of Glory, shed thy light.

Take us to our spoils tonight.

Flash out thy blaze, O skeleton hand,

And guide the feet of our trusty band.

Their faces were twisted and their mouths hung open, like they wanted to scream but nothing would come out. I saw Bunny's mama and daddy shuffling along. And there was the Green family too, their kids with no shoes on their feet. I saw J.D. Barnes and Otis Ross, their eyes wide open. There were the McGuires and the Wellingtons and other Hatcher family from across the river. They were all cursed.

"Give up, Hoodoo," Preacher Wellington said. "Give my master that hand. He's gonna call up the dead to stand against God's army."

That scared me more than anything. To see Preacher Wellington—a man of God—under the demon's spell just wasn't right.

I turned to see Aunt Jelly and Pa Manuel half running in my direction. They were both out of breath. Aunt Jelly was still in her robe. She didn't even have time to put on a dress. But they weren't going to stop me. I had to do this on my own. It was me Zacharias Cain wanted. I'd come this far, and I wasn't gonna let someone else finish it.

"Hoodoo!" Aunt Jelly cried.

"Stay back!" I shouted, raising my left hand.

Aunt Jelly and Pa Manuel stopped in their tracks. Pa Manuel looked at me like he was gonna say something, but then I saw him blow out a breath and tighten his lips.

Zacharias Cain began to chant, coming closer on his big black horse.

I am the darkness in the night . . .

Clip, clop, clip, clop.

I am the shadow before the sun . . .

Clip, clop, clip, clop.

I am the snake that walks with two legs . . .

Clip, clop, clip, clop.

My bones shook in my pants. The heat from my hand was rising all the way up my arm. I clenched it into a fist and whispered,

> *Saint Michael the Archangel, defend me in battle.*
>
> *Be my defense against the wickedness and snares of the devil.*
>
> *May God rebuke him, I humbly pray, and do thou,*
>
> *O Prince of the heavenly hosts, by the power of God,*
>
> *thrust into hell Satan, and all the evil spirits,*
>
> *who prowl about the world seeking the ruin of souls.*
>
> *Amen.*

I let out a breath. "Zacharias Cain!" I shouted. "Go away! Get out of here, you old demon!"

And then I waited. But for what, I didn't know. A bolt of lightning to strike him down? A hole to open up in the ground and swallow him? But neither of those things happened. The Stranger just chuckled, deep and low. "Gimme that hand, boy."

Aunt Jelly opened her mouth to scream but I didn't hear it. Time slowed down. I felt like I was standing in molasses, sinking down into the earth. Zacharias Cain was closer now—so close I felt the heat from his body drifting toward me. "You can't stop the night," he said. "Darkness is coming."

The wind rose up. I covered my nose with my hand as the smell of a dead skunk filled my nostrils. It was Zacharias Cain, stinking up the street to high heaven. "No!" I shouted. "Stay back!"

"What you gonna do, boy?" he said. "I will take that hand and then I will *EAT YOUR HEART!*"

I heard a bell, and it rang three times, soft and far away, like the bell I heard when I was soul traveling, talking to Daddy.

You gotta use your head, son, and your heart.

Mrs. Snuff said something like that too, and I heard her voice loud and clear:

Where'd you get that mark, boy? . . . Gotta have heart. Gotta have heart.

I heard a sound inside my head, like a heart beating in time with my real heart. I let out a deep breath, then raised my left hand and touched my birthmark. Heat spread through my fingertips. I brought my hand down and looked at it.

I gasped.

My left hand glowed, like it had been dipped in moonlight. I stared but didn't have time to wonder how or why. I just had to use it somehow.

My breath was coming fast. Blood rushed in my temples. My left hand was heavy now, like I was carrying around a hammer.

I thought back to everything that had brought me here: the mojo bag, the Saint Michael prayer, the powwow book, the Sator Square.

The Sator Square.

Cipher and speak the Sator Square. The evil that draws nigh is vanquished.

Vanquish means to defeat somebody, if you didn't know.

If those words had the power to show me the Stranger's true name, maybe they could do more.

Zacharias Cain drew closer. "*You* owe me a debt," he said. "And I come to collect."

I raised my glowing hand. "Sator!" I shouted.

Zacharias Cain twitched, then cocked his head sideways.

"Arepo!" I said. "Tenet!"

Something was happening. Zacharias Cain shook his head, like he wanted to speak but couldn't.

"Opera!"

The glow from my hand lit up the darkness. The townsfolk shrunk back, fear on their faces.

"Zacharias Cain!" I called out, and the voice that came out

of me was strong and deep. "Down in the valley you dwell. Five hundred steps. Go back to where you came from!"

His eyes flashed for a second—red and orange flames flickering in the shadows. His devil horse reared on its hind legs and threw him off, then bolted down the street, its hooves pounding the dirt road.

But in the blink of an eye, Zacharias Cain stood up and unfolded his legs like some kind of nasty insect, then ran at me, sickle in hand. He was on me in a second, his sharp knees pinning me to the ground. The townsfolk around me stood still and chanted.

Oh, Hand of Glory, shed thy light.

Take us to our spoils tonight.

"I will kill you, boy," he said, sparks flying out of his mouth. "Just like that old woman!" His face was inches from mine. The stench of the grave rolled over me, and I held my breath. He was too heavy. He grabbed my left wrist and held it to the ground, then raised his sickle. A cold blue light swirled around the blade. I shook my head back and forth, trying everything I could to loosen my arm, but his bony knees dug into my ribs, holding me in place.

I turned my head to see Bunny struggling like she wanted to speak. Her eyes bulged and her mouth opened up, but all that came out was nonsense words. I thought of everything in the world that had ever made me angry: J.D. Barnes and Otis Ross. Daddy, for trying to send his body into mine. Mama Frances sleeping in the cold, hard ground.

And just like that, my left hand shot out and grabbed Zacharias Cain around his neck.

I scrambled out from under him and stood up, holding his neck the whole while. I lifted him straight up off the ground, just like I did to J.D. Barnes, but now my hand was glowing like Saint Michael's holy sword. He kicked at the empty air, struggling and grunting

"Zacharias Cain!" I cried, looking him straight in the eye. "This is for my Mama Frances!"

"Rotas!" I shouted.

Big old balls of flame went up into Zacharias Cain's eyes and mouth. I drew my head back from the heat exploding from his face. I released my grip. The demon fell to the ground and raised his arms to the sky. Streaks of fire ran up his cloak. "I call on you, Great Master!" he cried. "Save your servant!"

And then the flames took him.

All was still.

Slowly, my breath came back to me. I looked at my left hand. The white light was gone. Bunny ran up and threw her arms around me. The townspeople shook their heads and turned in circles, dazed and confused, talking all in a rush. I looked into Bunny's eyes and held her. The smell of dandelions and sugar cane rose in my nostrils. "You did it, Hoodoo!" she cried. "You killed that old devil man!"

But I wasn't done yet. I had to make sure Zacharias Cain was really dead. I untangled myself and walked the few steps to his burned-up body. But as I stood over him, he dissolved into a pool of black worms, wriggling down into the earth.

TWENTY-SIX

Heart

The dark clouds overhead parted and the sun came out again. I heard birds whistling. Dirt streaked my pants and shirt. Bunny's mama scooped her up and headed down the street, back toward their house. I hoped they didn't think I was some kind of monster for what I'd just done.

I actually did it. I killed that old demon.

"Hoodoo!"

Aunt Jelly came running down the street, pulling her robe around her. She knelt and squeezed me in a big hug, then looked me up and down, touching my face, turning me around, and running her hands over my back like she was making sure I wasn't hurt. Pa Manuel was there, and Cousin Zeke, who looked fit to faint. I heard a rustling in the trees and looked up. It was that old black crow, hopping from branch to branch, making a racket.

And somebody else was there, too. A stooped and bent old lady, leaning on a knobby cane. She hobbled over and stood by Aunt Jelly.

"Miss Carter?" Aunt Jelly said.

I shook my head. *Miss Carter?* What was Aunt Jelly talking about? Her name was Mrs. Snuff.

"I got all kinds of names, boy," she said, answering my question before I even had a chance to ask it out loud. "Mrs. Snuff. Miss Carter. Addy. There's power in names. But I guess you know that now, don't you?"

"Yes ma'am," I said.

"You owe me two dollars and twenty-five cents for those things you took from my store," she said. "But I figure I can give you some credit."

She winked at me with her cloudy eye.

Aunt Jelly looked at us like we were both crazy. She reached out and held my face in her hands. "Fool child!" she said. "Let's get you home."

And then she tried to hug me again, and I went ahead and let her do it.

Try as he might to look all serious, Pa Manuel was proud of me, I could tell. He twirled his little cigar between his fingers, and the smoke swirled around his head. We were sitting at the dining room table, and Aunt Jelly made me a sweet drink of sugar water.

"How come you and Aunt Jelly didn't fall under the spell?" I asked him.

He took a sip of his drink and set the glass down on the table. "None of those families were hoodoo folk. That's why he was able to put that spell on them. He couldn't get in this house to take nothing."

Pa Manuel was right. Bunny's family didn't do folk magick, and neither did any of the other families that were under the Stranger's spell. I thought back to that night when I dreamed about the Stranger and how Mama Frances had put a broom across my doorway. And the altar must've helped.

We got the power of the Lord in this house. And other things too. It seemed like a long time ago now.

I swallowed and took a deep breath. "I went in the old Wise Men's club," I said. "I found something in there. Something that helped me get the Stranger's true name."

Aunt Jelly gave me a sharp look. "You know you shouldn't have gone in there, Hoodoo. No telling what kind of trouble you could've gotten into."

"Couldn't be more trouble than he already had," Pa Manuel said.

I had to smile at that a little, but I kept it inside.

"That lodge holds all kinds of secrets," Pa Manuel said. "Old books and spells, powerful magick from ages long gone."

"What happened to them?" I asked. "The Wise Men? Daddy was one of them. He was the boss, right?"

"Your daddy was the power behind that lodge," Pa Manuel said. "The youngest man ever to become the grand archon. Once he died, I'm afraid they fell into a shambles, son."

Pa Manuel stood up. He bent down and offered his hand. I reached out and shook it. It felt strange to shake my granddaddy's hand. He used to hug me when I was little, but I guessed I wasn't so little anymore. "What you did was brave, boy," he said. "Stupid, but brave." He straightened back up. "It takes a special kind of strength to stand up to evil like that. Way I see it, maybe one day you can start up that lodge again."

"Me?" I said.

"I reckon so."

I smiled at that, and so did Aunt Jelly.

Me, a Knight of the Wise Men. Figure that.

I sat with Bunny under a long-beard tree in the backyard. The moss hung so low it almost touched my head. Aunt Jelly had fried up a whole mess of catfish, and the soft, flaky meat melted in my mouth.

"I'm proud of you, Hoodoo," Bunny said. "I would've helped you if I could've. But I couldn't. I was . . . stuck."

I didn't ask her what it was like being under Zacharias Cain's spell—I just looked into her eyes and squeezed her hand. And then I leaned in and kissed her on the cheek. I wasn't even shy about it. And even though we'd both been eating fish and were hot from the sun, it was the sweetest kiss in the world.

"It's okay," I said. "You always believed in me. That's gotta count for something. Right?"

"Right," she said, and popped another piece of catfish in her mouth.

Aunt Jelly came out and filled our cups with sweet tea. She kept grinning at us like she had her own private joke.

I leaned back against the tree and crossed my hands behind my head. I thought about what I'd just gone through, and my daddy, too. He must be at peace now, I thought, and could enter the kingdom of heaven, like he said. And even though I was mad at him for what he did, in the end, it made me stronger. He told me I had to have heart, and I'd had it all the time.

Having heart is being brave, even when everything looks as dark as night.

Having heart is being strong, even when Zacharias Cain comes knocking.

Having heart is believing in yourself, if you didn't know.

ACKNOWLEDGMENTS

I would like to thank my parents, Henry and Rose Smith, for providing a childhood in which daydreams were easy and carefree, and not stifled by the concerns of the big, bad world. I found solace in books at an early age, and my parents always encouraged what would become a lifelong passion.

My brothers, Louis, Steven, and Calvin, always stalwart supporters, no matter what my endeavors. You guys are the best brothers one could wish for.

To my agent, Adriann Ranta, thanks for taking a chance on *Hoodoo* and believing in the book. You didn't have to ask for that initial revision, but I'm so thankful you did. Your support has been invaluable. (And thanks for having a patient ear in dealing with the neuroses of a debut author.)

To my editor, Lynne Polvino, at Clarion Books, thanks for

your critical eye and deft touch. You've helped me become a better writer. Also, I now know that the word "eye" cannot be used fifty-thousand times in a novel. (Even though I just used it twice.)

Thanks also to the marketing, publicity, and design teams at Houghton Mifflin Harcourt. You make me feel like An Important Author.

To Sebastian Skrobol, Cover Artist Extraordinaire, thanks for the brilliant cover.

I'd also like to give a special thanks to Michele Thornton and Amy Alexander Millay. One could not ask for more dedicated critique partners. This book would not have been possible without your insightful comments and suggestions. I hope to be reading your acknowledgment pages soon.

To my family and friends here and abroad, thanks for your unwavering support.

Lastly, to Julia, thanks for taking the journey with me. *Du bist die Liebe meines Lebens.*

ABOUT THE AUTHOR

Ronald L. Smith fell in love with books at a very young age and hasn't stopped reading since. *Hoodoo* is his debut novel, and he lives in Baltimore, Maryland. To learn more, please visit his website: www.strangeblackflowers.com.